AT CLOSE RANGE

"You're 'it.' I'll git the trunk at Kalamazoo."

AT
CLOSE RANGE

BY

F. HOPKINSON SMITH

ILLUSTRATED

CHARLES SCRIBNER'S SONS

NEW YORK :::::::::::::::::1905

TROW DIRECTORY
PRINTING AND BOOKBINDING COMPANY
NEW YORK

To my Readers:

On my writing-table lies a magnifying-glass the size of an old watch crystal, which helps me to understand the mechanism of many interesting things. With it I decipher at close range such finger-work as the cutting of intaglios, the brush-marks on miniatures, or perhaps the intricate fusings of metals in the sword-guard of a Samurai.

At the same close range I try to search the secret places of the many minds and hearts which in my nomadic life cross my path. In these magnifyings and probings the unexpected is ofttimes revealed: tenderness hiding behind suspected cruelty; refinement under assumed coarseness; the joy of giving forcing its way through thick crusts of pretended avarice.

The results confirm my theory, that at the bottom of every heart-crucible choked with life's cinders there can almost always be found a drop of gold.

F. H. S.

150 E. 34th Street, New York.

CONTENTS

ILLUSTRATIONS

A NIGHT OUT

A NIGHT OUT

THOREAU once spent the whole livelong night in the hush of the wilderness; sitting alone, listening to its sounds—the fall of a nut, the hoot of a distant owl, the ceaseless song of the frogs.

This night of mine was spent in the open; where men came and went and where the rush of many feet, and the babel of countless voices could be heard even in its stillest watches.

In my wanderings up and down the land, speaking first in one city and then in another, often with long distances between, I have had the good fortune to enjoy many such nights. Some of them are filled with the most delightful memories of my life.

.   .   .   .

The following telegram was handed me as I left the stage of the Opera House in Marshall, Mich., some months ago:

3

"Can you speak in Cleveland to-morrow afternoon at 2.30? Important.—Answer."

I looked at my watch. It was half past ten o'clock. Cleveland was two hundred miles away, and the Night Express to Toledo and the East, due in an hour, did not stop at Marshall.

I jumped into a hack, sprang out at the hotel entrance and corralled the clerk as he was leaving for the night. For some minutes we pored over a railway guide. This was the result:

Leave Marshall at 1.40 A.M., make a short run up the road to Battle Creek, stay there until half past three, then back again through Marshall without stopping, to Jackson—lie over another hour and so on to Adrian and Toledo for breakfast, arriving at Cleveland at 11.30 the next morning. An all-night trip, of course, with changes so frequent as to preclude the possibility of sleep, but a perfectly feasible one if the trains made reasonable time and connections.

This despatch went over the wires in reply:

"Yes, weather permitting."

To go upstairs and to bed and to be called in two

hours wouldn't pay for the trouble of undressing; better pick out the warm side of the stove, take two chairs and a paper two days old and kill time until one o'clock. I killed it alone—everybody having gone to sleep but the night porter, who was to telephone for the hack and assist with my luggage.

It was a silent night. One of those white, cold, silent nights when everything seems frozen—the people as well as the ground; no wind, no sounds from barking dogs or tread of hoof or rumble of wheels. A light snow was falling—an unnoticed snow, for the porter and I were the only people awake; at eleven o'clock a few whirling flakes; at twelve o'clock an inch deep, packed fine as salt, and as hard; at one o'clock three inches deep, smooth as a sheet and as unbroken; no furrow of wheels or slur of footstep. The people might have been in their graves and the snow their winding-shroud.

"Hack's ready, sir." This from the porter, rubbing his eyes and stumbling along with my luggage.

Into the hack again—same hack; it had been driven under the shed, making a night of it, too—

my trunk with a red band outside with the driver, my fur overcoat and grip inside with me.

There is nothing princely, now, about this coat; you wouldn't be specially proud of it if you could see it—just a plain fur overcoat—an old friend really—and still is. On cold nights I put it next to the frozen side of the car when I am lying in my berth. Often it covers my bed when the thermometer has dropped to zero and below, and I am sleeping with my window up. It has had experiences, too, this fur coat; a boy went home in it once with a broken leg, and his little sister rode with her arm around him, and once—but this isn't the place to tell about it.

From the hotel to the station the spools of the hack paid out two wabbly parallel threads, stringing them around corners and into narrow streets and out again, so that the team could find its way back, perhaps.

Another porter now met me—not sleepy this time, but very much awake; a big fellow in a jumper, with a number on his cap, who caught the red-banded trunk by the handle and "yanked" it (admirable word this!) on to the platform, shouting out in the same breath, "Cleveland via Battle Creek—no extras!"

Then came the shriek of the incoming train—a local bound for Battle Creek and beyond. Two cars on this train, a passenger and a smoker. I lugged the fur overcoat and grip up the snow-clogged steps and entered the smoker. No Pullman on these locals, and, of course, no porter, and travellers, therefore, did their own lifting and lugging.

The view down the perspective of this smoker was like a view across a battle-field, the long slanting lines of smoke telling of the carnage. Bodies (dead with sleep) were lying in every conceivable position, with legs and arms thrust up as if the victims had died in agony; some face down; others with gaping mouths and heads hooked across the seats. These heads and arms and legs made the passage of the aisle difficult. One—a leg—got tangled in my overcoat, and the head belonging to it said with a groan:

"Where in h— are you goin' with that——"

But I did not stop. I kept on my way to the passenger coach. It was not my fault that no Pullman with a porter attached was run on this local.

There was no smoke in this coach. Neither was there any heat. There was nothing that could cause it. Something had happened, perhaps to the coupling of the steam hose so that it wouldn't couple; or the bottom was out of the hollow mockery called a heater; or the coal had been held up. Whatever the cause, a freight shed was a palm garden beside it. Nor had it any signs of a battlefield. It looked more like a ward in a hospital with most of the beds empty. Only one or two were occupied; one by a baby and another by its mother— the woman on one seat, her hand across the body of the child, and both fast asleep, one little bare foot peeping out from beneath the shawl that covered the child, like a pink flower a-bloom in a desert.

I can always get along in a cold car. It is a hot one that incites me to murder the porter or the brakeman. I took off the coat I was wearing and laid it flat on a seat. Then came a layer of myself

Heads and arms and legs made the passage of the aisle difficult.

with the grip for a pillow, and then a top crust of my old friend. They might have knocked out the end of the car now and I should have been comfortable. Not to sleep—forty minutes wouldn't be of the slightest service to a night watchman, let alone an all-night traveller—but so as to be out of the way of porterless-passengers lugging grips.

The weather now took a hand in the game. The cold grew more intense, creeping stealthily along, blowing its frosty breath on the windows; so dense on some panes that the lights of the stations no longer shone clear, but were blurred, like lamps in a fog. The incoming passengers felt it and stamped their feet, shedding the snow from their boots. Now and then some traveller, colder than his fellow, stopped at the fraudulent heater to warm his fingers before finding a seat, and, strange to say, passed on satisfied—due to his heated imagination, no doubt.

The blanket of white was now six inches thick, and increasing every minute. The wind was still asleep.

"Guess we're in for it," said the conductor to a

ticket stuck in the hat of a man seated in front. "I hear No. 6 is stalled chuck-a-block this side of Schoolcraft. We'll make Battle Creek anyway, and as much furder as we can get, but there ain't no tellin' where we'll bring up."

I thrust my ticket hand through the crust of my overcoat and the steel nippers perforated the bit of cardboard with a click. I was undisturbed. Battle Creek was where I was to get off; what became of the train after that was no affair of mine.

Only one thing worried me as I lay curled up like a cocoon. Was there a hotel at Battle Creek within reasonable distance (walking, of course; no hack would be out a night like this), with a warm side to its stove and two more chairs in which I could pass the time of my stay, or would there be only the railroad station—and if the last, what sort of a railroad station?—one of those bare, varnished, steam-heated affairs with a weighing machine in one corner and a slot machine in the other? or a less modern chamber of horrors with the seats divided by iron arms—instruments of torture for tired, sleepy men which must have been devised in the Middle Ages?

The wind now awoke with a howl, kicked off its counterpane and started out on a career of its own. Ventilators began to rattle; incoming passengers entered with hands on their hats; outgoing passengers had theirs whipped from their heads before they touched the platforms of the stations. The conductor as he passed shook his head ominously:

" Goin' to be a ring-tailed roarer," he said to a man in the aisle whose face was tied up in a shawl with the ends knotted on top of his cap, like a boy with the toothache. "Cold enough to freeze the rivets in the b'iler. Be wuss by daylight."

" Will we make Battle Creek?" I asked, lifting my head from the grip.

"Yes; be there in two minutes. He's blowin' for her now."

Before the brakeman had tightened his clutch on his brake I was on my feet, had shifted overcoats, and was leaning against the fraudulent heater ready to face the storm.

It would have been a far-seeing eye that could

11

have discovered a hotel. All I saw as I dropped to the snow-covered platform was a row of gas jets, a lone figure pushing a truck piled up with luggage, one arm across his face to shield it from the cutting snow, and above me the gray mass of the station, its roof lost in the gloom of the wintry night. Then an unencumbered passenger, more active than I, passed me up the wind-swept platform, pushed open a door, and he and I stepped into— What did I step into? Well, it would be impossible for you to imagine, and so I will tell you in a new paragraph.

I stepped into a little gem of a station, looking like a library without its books, covered by a low roof, pierced by quaint windows and fitted with a big, deep, all-embracing fireplace ablaze with crackling logs resting on old-fashioned iron dogs, and beside them on the hearth a huge pile of birch wood. A room once seen never to be forgotten—a cosey box of a place, full of curved alcoves and half-round recesses with still smaller windows, and a table bearing a silver-plated ice-pitcher and two silver-plated goblets, *unchained* (really, I am telling the truth), and big easy chairs, five or six of them, some of wicker-work with cushions, and a straw lounge big enough and long enough to stretch out on at full length. All this, remember, from out a night savage as a pack of wolves, and quite a thousand miles from home.

I gravitated instinctively toward the fire, threw my overcoat and grip on the lounge and looked about me. The one passenger besides myself tarried long enough at the ticket office to speak to the clerk, and then passed on through the other door. He lived here, perhaps, or preferred the hotel—wherever that was—to the comforts of the station.

The ticket-clerk locked his office, looked over to where I stood with my back to the blazing fire, my eyes roving around the room, and called out:

"I'm going home now. Hotel's only three blocks away."

"When is the down train due?" I asked.

"Three-thirty."

"Will it be on time?"

"Never stole it. Search me! May be an hour late; may be two," he added with a laugh.

"I'll stay here, if you don't mind."

"Course—glad to have you. You'll want more wood, though. . . . John!"—this to the man who had been pushing the truck—" bring in some more wood; man's going to stay here for No. 8. Good-night." And he shut the door and went out into the storm, his coat-sleeve across his face.

John appeared and dropped an armful of clean split silver-backed birch logs in a heap on the hearth, remarking as he bobbed his head good-night, "Guess you won't freeze," and left by the same exit as the clerk, a breath of the North Pole being puffed into the cosey room as he opened and shut the door.

There are times when to me it is a delight to be left alone. I invariably experience it when I am sketching. I often have this feeling, too, when my study door is shut and I am alone with my work and books. I had it in an increased degree this night, with the snow drifting outside, the wind fingering around the windows seeking for an entrance, and the whole world sound asleep except myself. It seemed good to be alone in the white stillness.

14

A NIGHT OUT

What difference did the time of night make, or the place, or the storm, or the morrow and what it might bring, so long as I could repeat in a measure the comforts and privacy of my own dear den at home?

I began to put my house in order. The table with the pitcher and goblets was drawn up by the side of the sofa; two easy chairs moved into position, one for my feet and one for my back, where the overhanging electric light would fall conveniently, and another log thrown on the fire, sending the crisp blazing sparks upward. My fur overcoat was next hung over the chair with the fur side out, the grip opened, and the several comforts one always carries were fished out and laid beside the ice-pitcher—my flask of Private Stock, a collar-box full of cigars, some books and a bundle of proof with a special delivery stamp—proofs that should have been revised and mailed two days before. These last were placed within reach of my hand.

When all was in order for the master of the house to take his ease, I unscrewed the top of the flask, and with the help of the pitcher and the goblet compounded a comfort. Then I lighted a cigar and began a tour of the room. The windows were banked up with the drift; through the half-blinded panes I could see the flickering gas jets and on the snow below them the disks of white light. Beyond these stretched a ruling of tracks edged by a bordering of empty yard-cars, then a waste of white ending in gloom. The only sounds were the creaking of the depot signs swaying in the wind and the crackle of the logs on my hearth—*mine* now in the isolation, as was everything else about me. Next I looked between the wooden spindles of the fenced-in ticket office, and saw where the clerk worked and how he kept his pens racked up and the hook on which he hung his hat and coat, and near it the news-stand locked tight, only the book posters showing over the top, and so on back to my fire and into my fur-lined throne. Then, with a sip of P. S., I picked up my proof sheets and began to work.

Before I had corrected my first galley my ear caught the sound of stamping feet outside. Some early train-hand, perhaps, or porter, or some passenger who had misread the schedule; for nothing up or down was to pass the station except, perhaps, a belated freight. Then the door was burst open, and a voice as crisp as the gust of wind that ushered it in called out:

"Well, begorra! ye look as snug as a bug in a rug. What d'ye think of this for a night?"

He was approaching the fire now, shaking the snow from his uniform and beating his hands together as he walked.

I have a language adapted to policemen and their kind, and I invariably use it when occasion offers. Strange to say, my delight at being alone had now lost its edge.

"Corker, isn't it?" I answered. "Draw up a chair and make yourself comfortable."

"Well, I don't care if I do. By Jiminy! I thought the ears of me would freeze as I come acrost the yard. What are ye waitin' for—the 3.30?"

"I am. Here, take a nip of this," and I handed him the other goblet and pushed the P. S. his way. Corrupting the Force, I know, but then consider the temptation, and the fact that I was stranded on a

17

lone isle of the sea, or adrift on a detached ice floe (that's a better simile), and he the only other human being within reach.

He raised the flask to his eye, noted the flow line, poured out three fingers, added one finger of water, said "How!" and emptied the mixture into his person. Then I handed him a cigar, laid aside my proofs and began to talk. I not only had a fire and a pile of wood, with something to smoke and enough P. S. for two, but I had a friend to enjoy them with me. Marvellous place—this Battle Creek!

"Anything doing?" I asked after the storm and the night had been discussed and my lighted match had kindled his cigar.

"Only a couple o' drunks lyin' outside a j'int," he answered, stretching his full length in the chair.

"Did you run 'em in?"

"No, the station was some ways, so I tuk 'em inside. I know the feller that runs the j'int an' the back dure was open—" and he winked at me. "They'd froze if I'd left 'em in the drift. Wan had the ears of him purty blue as it wuz."

"Anything else?"

18

A NIGHT OUT

"Well, there was a woman hollerin' bloody murther back o' the lumber yard, but I didn't stop to luk her up. They're allus raisin' a muss up there —it was in thim tiniments. Ye know the place." (He evidently took me for a resident or a rounder.) "Guess I'll be joggin' 'long" (here he rose to his feet), "my beat's both sides of the depot an' I daren't stop long. Good luck to ye."

"Will you drop in again?"

"Yes, maybe I will," and he opened the door and stepped out, his hand on his cap as the wind struck it.

Half an hour passed.

Then the cough of a distant locomotive, catching its breath in the teeth of the gale, followed by the rumbling of a heavily loaded train, growing louder as it approached, could be heard above the wail of the storm.

When it arrived off my window I rose from my seat and looked out through the blurred glass. The breast of the locomotive was a bank of snow, the fronts and sides of the cars were plastered with the drift. The engineer's head hung out of the cab win-

19

dow, his eye on the swinging signal lights. Huddling close under the lee of the last box car I caught the outline of a brakeman, his cap pulled over his ears, his jacket buttoned tight. The train passed without stopping, the cough of the engine growing fainter and fainter as it was lost in the whirl of the gale. I regained my seat, lighted another cigar and picked up my proofs again.

Another half hour passed. The world began to awake.

First came the clerk with a cheery nod; then the man who had brought in the wood and who walked straight toward the pile to see how much of it was left and whether I needed any more; then the lone passenger who had gone to the hotel and who was filled to the bursting point with profanity, and who emitted it in blue streaks of swear-words because of his accommodations; and last the policeman, beating his chest like a gorilla, the snow flying in every direction.

The circle widened and another log was thrown on the crackling fire. More easy chairs were drawn up, the policeman in one and the clerk in another.

Then the same old pantomime took place over the
P. S. and the goblets, and the old collar-box had
its lid lifted and did its duty bravely. The lone
passenger, being ill-tempered and out of harmony
with the surroundings, was not invited. (What
a lot of fun the ill-tempered miss in this world of
care!)

Some talk of the road now followed, whether the
Flyer would get through to Chicago, the clerk remarking that No. 8 ought to arrive at 3.30, as it
was a local and only came from Kalamazoo. Talk,
too, of how long I would have to wait at Jackson,
and what accommodations the train had, the clerk
in an apologetic voice remarking, as he sipped his
P. S., that it was a "straight passenger," with nothing aboard that would suit *me*. Talk of the town,
the policeman saying that the woman was "bilin'
drunk" and he had to run both her and the old man
in before the "tiniment got quiet," the lone passenger interpolating from his seat by the steam
pipes that— But it's just as well to omit what the
lone passenger said, or this paper would never see
the light.

AT CLOSE RANGE

At 3.30 the clerk sprang from his chair. He had, with his quick ear, caught the long-drawn-out shriek of No. 8 above the thrash of the storm.

Into my overcoat again, in a hurry this time—everybody helping—the fur one, of course, the other on my arm—a handshake all round, out again into the whirl, the policeman carrying the grip; up a slant of snow on the steps of the cars—not a traveller's foot had yet touched it, and into an ordinary passenger coach: all in less than two minutes—less time, in fact, than it would take to shift the scenery in a melodrama, and with as startling results.

No sleeping corpses here sprawled over seats, with arms and legs thrust up; no mothers watched their children; no half-frozen travellers shivered beside ice-cold heaters. The car was warm, the lights burned cheerily, the seats were unlocked and faced both ways.

Not many passengers either—only six besides myself at my end. Three of them were wearing picture hats the size of tea-trays, short skirts, and high shoes with red heels. The other three wore

Derbies and the unmistakable garb of the average drummer. Each couple had a double seat all to themselves, and all six were shouting with laughter. Packed in the other end of the car were the usual collection of travellers seen on an owl train.

I passed on toward the middle of the coach, turned a seat, and proceeded to camp for the night. The overcoat did service now as a seat cushion and the grip as a rest for my elbow.

It soon became evident that the girls belonged to a troupe on their way to Detroit; that they had danced in Kalamazoo but a few hours before, had supped with the drummers, and had boarded the train at 2.50. As their conversation was addressed to the circumambient air, there was no difficulty in my gaining these facts. If my grave and reverend presence acted as a damper on their hilarity, there was no evidence of it in their manner.

"Say, Liz," cried the girl in the pink waist, "did you catch on to the—" Here her head was tucked under the chin of the girl behind her.

"Oh, cut it out, Mame!" answered Liz. "Now, George, you stop!" This with a scream at one of the drummers, whose head had been thrust close to Mame's ear in an attempt to listen.

"Say, girls," broke in another—they were all talking at once—"why, them fellers in the front seat went on awful! I seen Sanders lookin' and—"

" Well, what if he *did* look? That guy ain't—" etc., etc.

I began to realize now why the other passengers were packed together in the far end of the car. I broke camp and moved down their way.

The train sped on. I busied myself studying the loops and curls of snow that the eddying wind was piling up in the cuts and opens, as they lay glistening under the glow of the lights streaming through the car windows; noting, too, here and there, a fence post standing alone where some curious wind-fluke had scooped clear the drifts.

Soon I began to speculate on the outcome of the trip. I had at best only three hours leeway between 11.30 A.M., the schedule time of arriving in Cleveland, and 2.30 P.M., the hour of my lecture— not much in a storm like this, with every train delayed and the outlook worse every hour.

A NIGHT OUT

At Albion the drummers got out, the girls waving their hands at them through the frosted windows. When the jolly party of coryphées regained their seats, their regulation smiles, much to my surprise, had faded. Five minutes later, when I craned my neck to look at them, wondering why their boisterousness had ceased, the three had wrapped themselves up in their night cloaks and were fast asleep. The drummers, no doubt, forgot them as quickly.

The conductor now came along and shook a sleepy man on the seat behind me into consciousness. He had a small leather case with him and looked like a doctor—was, probably; picked up above Battle Creek, no doubt, by a hurry call. He had been catching a nap while he could. Jackson was ten minutes away, so the conductor told the man.

More stumbling down the snow-choked steps and plunging through drifts (it was too early yet for the yard shovellers), and I entered the depot at Jackson—my second stop on the way to Cleveland.

No cry of delight escaped my lips as I pushed open the door. The Middle Ages have it all their own way at Jackson and still do unless the Battle Creek architect has since modernized the building. Nothing longer than a poodle or a six months' old baby could stretch its length on these iron-divided seats. "Move on" must have been the watchword, for nobody sat—not if they could help it. I tried it, spreading the overcoat between two of them, but the iron soon entered my soul, or rather my hip joints, and yet I am not over large. No open wood fire, of course, no easy chairs, no lounge; somebody might pass a few minutes in comfort if there were. There was a sign, I remember, nailed up, reading "No loiterers allowed here," an utterly useless affair, for nobody that I saw *loitered*. They "skedaddled" at once (that's another expressive word, old as it is), and they failed to return until the next train came along. Then they gathered for a moment and again disappeared. No, the station building at Jackson is not an enticing place—not after Battle Creek.

And yet I was not unhappy. I had only an hour to wait—perhaps two—depending on the way the tracks were blocked.

A NIGHT OUT

I unlocked the grip. There was nothing left of the P. S.—the policeman had seen to that; and the collar-box was empty—the clerk had had a hand in that—two, if I remember. The proofs were finished and ready to mail, and so I buttoned up my fur coat and went out into the night again in search of the post-box, tramping the platform where the wind had swept it clean. The crisp air and the sting of the snow-flakes felt good to me.

Soon my eye fell on a lump tied up with rope and half-buried in the snow. The up-train from Detroit had thrown out a bundle of the morning edition of the Detroit papers. I lugged it inside the station, brushed off the snow, dragged it to a seat beneath a flaring gas jet, cut the rope with my knife and took out two copies damp with snow. I was in touch with the world once more, whatever happened! I soon forgot the hardness of the seat and only became conscious that someone had entered the room when a voice startled me with:

"Say, Boss!"

I looked up over my paper and saw a boy with his head tied up in an old-fashioned tippet. He

27

was blowing his breath on his fingers, his cheeks like two red apples.

"Well, what is it?"

"How many poipers did ye swipe?"

"Oh, are you the newsboy? Do these belong to you?"

"You bet! How many ye got?"

"Two."

"Ten cents, Boss. Thank ye," and he shouldered the bundle and went out into the night, where a wagon was standing to receive it.

"Level-headed boy," I said to myself. "Be a millionaire if he lives. No back talk, no unnecessary remarks regarding an inexcusable violation of the law—petty larceny if anything. Just a plain business statement, followed by an immediate cash settlement. A most estimable boy."

A road employee now came in, looked at the dull-faced clock on the wall, went out through a door and into a room where a telegraph instrument was clicking away, returned with a piece of chalk and wrote on a black-board:

"No. 31—52 minutes late."

A NIGHT OUT

This handwriting on the wall had a Belshazzar-feast effect on me. If I lost the connection at Adrian, what would become of the lecture in Cleveland?

Another man now entered carrying a black carpet-bag—a sleepy man with his hair tousled and who looked as if he had gone to bed in his clothes. He fumbled in his pocket for a key, went straight to the slot machine, unlocked it, disclosing a reduced stock of chewing-gum and chocolate caramels, opened his carpet-bag and filled the machine to the top. This sort of a man works at night, I thought, when few people are about. To uncover the mysteries of a slot machine before a gaping crowd would be as foolish and unprofitable as for a conjurer to show his patrons how he performed his tricks.

I became conscious now, even as I turned the sheets of the journal, that while my flask of P. S. and the contents of my collar-box were admirable in their place, they were not capable of sustaining life, even had both receptacles been full, which they were not. There was evidently nothing to eat in the station, and from what I saw of the outside, no one had yet started a fire; no one had even struck a light.

At this moment a gas jet flashed its glare through a glass door to my right. I had seen this door, but supposed it led to the baggage-room—a fact that did not concern me in the least, for I had checked my red-banded trunk through to Cleveland. I got up and peered in. A stout woman in a hood, with a blanket shawl crossed over her bosom, its ends tied behind her back, was busying herself about a nickel-plated coffee-urn decorating one end of a long counter before which stood a row of high stools—the kind we sat on in school. I tried the knob of the door and walked in.

"Is this the restaurant?"

"What would ye take it for—a morgue?" she snapped out.

"Can I get a cup of coffee?"

"No, ye can't, not till six o'clock. And ye won't git it then if somebody don't turn out to help. Sittin' up all night lally-gaggin' and leavin' a pile o' dirty dishes for me to wash up. Look at 'em!"

A NIGHT OUT

"Who's sitting up?" I inquired in a mild voice.

"These *'ladies'* "—this with infinite scorn— "that's doin' waitin' for six dollars a week and what they kin pick up, and it's my opinion they picks up more'n 's good for 'em."

"And they make you do all the work?"

"Well, ye'd think so if ye stayed 'round here."

"Can I help?"

She had been swabbing down the counter as she talked, accentuating every sentence with an extra twist of her arm, the wash-cloth held tight between her fingers. She stopped now and looked me squarely in the face.

"*Help!* What are *you* good for?" There was a tone of contempt in her voice.

"Well, I'm handy passing plates and cutting bread and pie. I've nothing to do till the train comes along. Try me a while."

"You don't look like no waiter."

"But I am. I've been waiting on people all my life." I had crawled under the counter now and was standing beside her. "Where will you have this?" and I picked up from a side table a dish of

31

apples and oranges caged in a wire screen. I knew
I was lost if I hesitated.

"Lay 'em here," she answered without a word of
protest. I was not surprised. The big and bound-
less West has no place for men ashamed to work
with their hands. Only the week before, in Colorado
Springs, I had dined at a house where the second
son of a noble lord had delivered the family milk
that same morning, he being the guest of honor.
And then—I was hungry.

The woman watched me put the finishing touches
on the dish of fruit, and said in an altered tone, as
if her misgivings had been satisfied:

"Now, fill that bucket with water, will ye? The
sink's behind ye. I'll start the coffee. And *here!*"
and she handed me a key—"after ye fetch the
water, unlock the refrigerator and bring me that
ham and them baked beans."

Before the "ladies" had arrived—half an hour,
in fact, before one of them had put in an appearance—I was seated at a small table covered with
a clean cloth (I had set the table) with half a ham,
a whole loaf of bread, a pitcher of milk that had

been left outside in the snow and was full of lovely ice crystals, a smoking cup of coffee and a smoking pile of griddle cakes which the woman had compounded from the contents of two paper packages, and which she herself had cooked on a gas griddle —and very good cakes they were: total cost, as per schedule, fifty cents.

Breakfast over, I again sought the seclusion of the Torture Chamber. The man with the piece of chalk had been kept busy. No. 31 was now one hour and forty-two minutes late.

When it finally reached Jackson and I boarded it with my grip and overcoat, it looked as if it had run into a glacier somewhere up the road and had half a snowslide still clinging to its length.

Day had broken now, and what light could sift its way through the falling flakes, shone cold and gray into the frost-dimmed windows of the car. I had lost more than two hours of my leeway of three, and the drifts were still level with the hubs of the driving-wheels.

We shunted and puffed and jerked along, waiting on side tracks for freight trains hours behind time and switching out of the way of delayed "Flyers," and finally reached Adrian. (Does anybody know of a Flyer that is on time when but a bare inch of snow covers the track?)

Out of the car again, still lugging my impedimenta.

"Train for Toledo and the East, did you say?" answered the ticket agent. "Yes, No. 32 is due in ten minutes—she's way behind time and so you've just caught her. Your ticket is good, but you can't carry no baggage."

The information came as a distinct shock. No baggage meant no proper habiliments in which to appear before my distinguished and critical audience—the most distinguished and critical which I ever had the good fortune to address—a young ladies' school.

"Why no baggage?"

"'Cause there's nothing but Pullmans, and only express freight carried—it's a news train. Ought to have been here a week ago."

"Can I give up my check and send my trunk by express?"

A NIGHT OUT

"Yes. That's the agent over there by the radiator."

One American dollar accomplished it—a silver one; they don't use any other kind of money out West.

When No. 32 hove in sight—the Fast Mail is its proper name—and stopped opposite the small station at Adrian, a blessed, beloved, be-capped, be-buttoned and be-overcoated Pullman porter—an attentive, considerate, alert porter—emerged from it and at a sign from me picked up my overcoat and grip—they now weighed a ton apiece—and with a wave of his hand conducted me into a well-swept, well-ordered Pullman.

"Porter, what's your name?" I inquired. (I always ask a porter his name.)

"Samuel Thomas, sah."

"Sam, is there a berth left?"

"Yes, sah—No. 9 lower."

"Is it in order?"

"Yes, sah—made up for a gem'man at South Bend, but he didn't show up."

"Let me see it."

It was exactly as he had stated; even the upper berth was clewed up.

"Sam!"

"Yes, sah."

"Are you married?"

"Yes, sah."

"Got any children?"

"Yes, sah—two."

"Think a good deal of them?"

"Yes, sah." The darky was evidently at sea now.

"Well, Sam, I'm going to bed and to sleep. If anybody disturbs me until we get within fifteen minutes of Cleveland, your family will never see you alive again. Do you understand, Sam?"

"Yes, sah, I understand." His face was in a broad grin now. "Thank ye, sah. Here's an extra pillow," and he drew the curtains about me.

.   .   .   .

At twenty-five minutes past two, and with five minutes to spare, I stepped on to the platform of the Academy for Young Ladies in Cleveland, properly clothed and in my right mind.

The "weather had permitted."

36

AN EXTRA BLANKET

AN EXTRA BLANKET

STEVE was angry.

You could see that from the way he strode up and down the platform of the covered railroad station, talking to himself in staccato explosives, like an automobile getting under way. Steve had lost his sample trunk; and a drummer without his trunk is as helpless as a lone fisherman without bait.

Outside, a snow-storm was working itself up into a blizzard; cuts level with the fences, short curves choked with drifts, flat stretches bare of a flake. Inside, a panting locomotive crawled ahead of two Pullmans and a baggage—a Special from Detroit to Kalamazoo, six hours late, loaded with comic-opera people, their baggage, properties—and Steve's lost trunk.

When the train pulled up opposite to where

39

Steve stood, the engine looked like a snow-plough that had burrowed through a drift.

Steve moved down to the step of the first Pullman, his absorbing eye taking in the train, the fragments of the drift, and the noses of the chorus girls pressed flat against the frosted panes. The conductor was now on the platform, crunching a tissue telegram which the station-master had just handed him. He had stopped for orders and for a wider breathing space, where he could get out into the open and stretch his arms, and become personal and perhaps profane without wounding the feelings of his passengers.

Steve stepped up beside him and showed him an open telegram.

"Yes, your trunk's aboard all right," replied the conductor, "but I couldn't find it in a week. A lot of scenery and ladders and truck all piled in. I am sorry, but I wouldn't——"

"What you 'wouldn't,' my sweet Aleck, don't interest me," exploded Steve. "You get a couple of porters and go through that stuff and find my trunk, or I'll wire the main office that——"

40

AN EXTRA BLANKET

"See here, young feller. Don't get gay. Hit that gourd of yours another crack and maybe you'll knock some sense into it. We're six hours late, ain't we? We got three hours to make Kalamazoo in, ain't we? This show's got to get there on time, or there'll be H to pay and no pitch hot. Now go outside and stand in a door somewheres and let the wind blow through you. I'll wire you in the morning, or you can take the 5.40 and pick your trunk up at Kalamazoo.—Let her go, Johnny"—this to the engine-driver. "All aboard!"

Steve jerked a cigar from his waistcoat pocket, cut off the end, and said, with a bite-in-two-ten-penny-nail expression about his lips:

"Steve, you're 'it.' I'll git that trunk at Kalamazoo."

Then he crossed the platform, made his way to the street entrance, and stepped into the omnibus of the only hotel in the town.

When the swinging sign of the Two-dollar House, blurred in the whirl of the storm, hove in sight, Steve's face was still knotted in wrinkles. He had a customer in this town good for three hundred dozen table cutlery, and but for "this gang of cross-tie steppers," he said to himself, he would . . . Here the hind heels of the 'bus hit the curb, cutting short Steve's anathema.

The drummer picked up his grip and made his way to the desk.

"What's the matter, Stevey?" asked Larry, the clerk. "You look sour."

"Sour? I am a green pickle, Larry, that's what I am—a green pickle. Been waiting five hours for my trunk in that oriental palm garden of yours you call a station. It was aboard a Special loaded with chorus girls and props. Conductor wouldn't dump it, and now it's gone on to Kalamazoo and——"

"Oh, but you'll get it all right. All you've got to do, Steve, is to——"

"Get it! Yes, when the daisies are blooming over us. I want it *now*, Larry. Whenever I run up against anything solid it's always one of these fly-by-nights. What do you think of going upstairs in the dark and hauling out a red silk hat and a pair of gilt slippers, instead of a sample card of

42

carvers? Well, that's what a guy did for me last fall down at Logansport. Sent me two burial caskets full of chorus-girl props instead of my trunk. Oh, yes, I'll *get* it—get it in the neck. Here, send this grip to my room."

The clerk pursed his lips and looked over his key-rack. He knew that he had no room—none that would suit Stephen Dodd—had known it when he saw him entering the door, the snow covering his hat and shoulders, his grip in his hands.

"Going to stay all night with us, Stephen?" Larry asked.

"Sure! What do you think I'm here for? Blowing and snowing outside fit to beat the band. What do you want me to do—bunk in the station?"

"H'm, h'm," muttered the clerk, studying the key-rack and name-board as if they were plans of an enemy's country.

Steve looked up. When a clerk began to say "H'm," Steve knew something was wrong.

"Full?"

"Well, not exactly full, Steve, but—h'm—we've

got the 'Joe Gridley Combination' with us over-night, and about everything——"

"Go on—go on—what'd I tell you? Up ag'in these fly-by-nights as usual!" blurted out Steve.

The clerk raised his hand deprecatingly.

"Sorry, old man. Put you on the top floor with some of the troupe—good rooms, of course, but not what I like to give you. Leading lady's got your room, and the manager's got the one you sometimes have over the extension. It'll only be for to-night. They're going away in the morning, and I——"

"Cut it out—cut it out—and forget it," interrupted Steve. "So am I going away in the morning. Got to take the 5.40 and hunt up that trunk. Can't do a thing without it. Only waltzed in here to get something to eat and a bed. Be back later. Put me anywhere. This week's hoodooed, and these show guys are doing it. You want a guardian, Stephen —a gentle, mild-eyed little guardian. That's what you want."

The clerk rang a gong that sounded like a fire-alarm and the porter came in on a run.

44

AN EXTRA BLANKET

"Take Mr. Dodd's grip and show him up to Number 11."

On the way upstairs Steve's quick eye caught the flare of a play-bill tacked to one wall.

"What is it?" he asked of the porter, pointing to the poster—"an 'East Lynne' or a 'Mother's Curse'?"

"No—one o' them mix-ups, I guess. Song and dance stunts. Number 11, did Larry say? There ye are—key's in the lock." And the porter pushed open the door of the room with his foot, dropped Steve's bag on the pine table, turned up the gas—the twilight was coming on—asked if there was "anything more"—found there wasn't—not even a dime—and left Steve in possession.

" 'Bout as big as a coffin, and as cold," grumbled Steve, looking around the room. "No steam-heat—one pillow and"—here he punched the bed—"one blanket, and thin at that—the bed hard as a—Well, if this don't take the cake! If this burg don't get a hotel soon I'll cut it out of my territory."

Steve washed his hands; wiped them on a 14x20 towel; hung it flat, that it might dry and be use-

45

ful in the morning, gave his hair a slick with his comb, scooped up a dozen cigars from a paper box, stuffed them in his outside pocket, relocked his grip, and retraced his steps downstairs.

When he reached the play-bill again he stopped for particulars. Condensed and pruned of inflammatory adjectives, the gay-colored document conveyed the information that the "Joe Gridley Combination" would play for this one night, performance beginning at 8 p.m., sharp. Molly Martin and Jessie Hannibal would dance, Jerry Gobo, the clown, would dislocate the ribs of the audience by his mirth-provoking sallies, and Miss Pearl Rogers of International, etc., etc., would charm them by her up-to-date delineations of genteel society. Then followed a list of the lesser lights, including chorus girls, clog dancers, and acrobats.

The porter was now shaking the red-hot stove with a cast-iron crank the size and shape of a burglar's jimmy, the ashes falling on a square of zinc protecting the uncarpeted floor. Steve recognized the noise, and looking down over the handrail called out, pointing to the poster:

46

AN EXTRA BLANKET

" How far's this shebang?"

" 'Bout a block."

"That settles it," said Steve to himself in the only contented tone of voice he had used since he entered the hotel. "I'll take this in." And continuing on downstairs, he dropped into a chair, completing the circle around the dispenser of comfort.

The business of the hotel went on. Trains arrived and were met by the lumbering stage, the passengers landing in the snow on the sidewalk—some for supper, one or two for rooms.

Supper was announced by a tight-laced blonde in white muslin, all hips and shoulders, throwing open the dining-room and mounting guard at the entrance, her face illumined by that knock-a-chip-off-my-shoulder expression common to her class.

Instantly, and with a simultaneous scraping of chair legs, the segments of the circle around the stove flung themselves into the narrow passageway.

Soon the racks were spotted with hats, their owners being drawn up in fours around the several tables—Steve one of them—the waiter-ladies serv-

47

ing with a sweetness of smile and elegance of manner found nowhere outside of a royal court, accompanied by a dignity of pose made all the more distinguished by a certain inward scoop of the back and instantaneous outward bulge below the waist line seen only in wax figures flanking a cloak counter.

Steve had a steak, liver and bacon, apple pie, a cup of coffee, and a toothpick—all in ten minutes. Then he resumed his place by the stove, lit a cigar, and kept his eye on the clock.

Three hours later Steve was again in his chair by the stove. He had been to the show and had sat through two hours of the performance. If his expression had savored of vinegar over the loss of his sample trunks, it was now double-proof vitriol!

"Thought you was goin' to the show," grunted the porter between his jerks at the handle; he was again at the stove, the thermometer marking zero outside.

"Been. Regular frost; buncoed out of fifty cents! That show is the limit! A couple of skinny-legged

48

girls doing a clog stunt; a bag of bones in a low-necked dress playing Mrs. Langtry; and a wall-eyed clown that looked like a grave-digger. Rotten—worst I ever saw!"

"Full house?"

"Full of empties. 'Bout fifty people, I guess, counting deadheads—and ME."

Steve accentuated this last word as if his fifty cents had been the only real income of the house.

The outer door now opened, letting in a section of the north pole and a cough.

Steve twisted around in his chair and recognized Jerry Goho, the clown. His grease paint was gone, but his haggard features and the graveyard hack settled his identity.

Jerry loosened the collar of his frayed, almost threadbare coat, approached the stove slowly, and stretching out one blue, emaciated hand, warmed it for an instant at its open door—in an apologetic way—as if the warming of one hand was all that he was entitled to.

Steve absorbed him at a glance. He saw that his neck was thin, especially behind the ears, the cords

49

of the throat showing; his cheeks sunken; the sad, kindly eyes peering out at him furtively from under bushy eyebrows, bright and glassy; his knees, too, seemed unsteady. As he stood warming his chilled fingers, his hand and arm extended toward the heat, his body drawn back, Steve got the impression of a boy reaching out for an apple, and ready to cut and run at the first alarm.

"Kind o' chilly," the clown ventured, in a voice that came from somewhere below his collar-button.

"Yes," said Steve gruffly. He didn't intend to start any conversation. He knew these fellows. One had done him out of eleven dollars in a ten-cent game up at Logansport the winter before. That particular galoot didn't have a cough, but he would have had if he could have doubled his winnings by it.

Jerry, rebuffed by Steve's curt reply, brought up the other hand, toasted it for an instant at the kindly blaze, rubbed the two sets of bony knuckles together, and remarking—this time to himself— that he "guessed he'd turn in," walked slowly to the foot of the stairs and began ascending the long

flight, his progress up one wall and half around
the next marked by his fingers sliding along the
hand-rail. Steve noticed that the bunched knuckles
stopped at the first landing (it was all that he could
see from where he sat), and after a spell of coughing slid slowly on around the court.

The drummer bit off the end of a fresh cigar;
scraped a match on the under side of his chair seat;
lit the domestic, and said with his first puff of
smoke, his mind still on the emaciated form of
the clown:

"Kindlin' wood for a new crematory."

Again the outer door swung open.

This time the Walking Lady entered, accompanied by the Business Agent. She wore a long
brown cloak that came to her feet and a stringy fur
tippet, her head and face covered by a hat concealed in a thick blue veil. This last she unwound
inside the hall, and seeing Steve monopolizing the
stove, began the ascent of the stairs, one step at a
time, as if she was tired out.

Steve turned his face away. The bag of bones
looked worse than ever. " 'Bout fifty in the shade,

I should think," he said to himself. "Ought to be taking in washing and ironing." Meantime Mathews, the Business Agent, was occupied with the clerk—Larry had presented him with a bill. The rates, the agent pleaded, were to be a dollar-sixty. Larry insisted on two dollars. Steve pricked up his ears; this interested him. If Larry wanted any backing as to the price he was within call. This information he conveyed to Larry by lifting his chin and slowly closing his left eye.

The outer door continued its vibrations with the rapidity of its green-baize namesake leading from the dining-room to the kitchen, ushering in some member of the troupe with every swing, including an elderly woman who had played the Duchess in the first act and a fishwife in the second; some young men with their hats over their noses, and four or five chorus girls. The men looked around for the index hand showing the location of the bar, and the girls, after a fit of giggling, began the ascent of the stairs to their rooms. Steve noticed that two of them continued on to the third floor, where Jerry Gobo, the clown, had gone, and where he him-

Some young men .   .   .   and four or five chorus girls.

self was to sleep. One of the girls looked down at him as she turned the corner of the stairs and nudged her companion—all of which was lost on the drummer. They had probably recognized him in the audience.

Nothing, however, in their present make-up could have recalled them to Steve's memory. Molly Martin had exchanged her green silk tights and gauze wings for a red flannel shirt-waist, a black leather belt, blue skirt, and cat-skin jacket. And Jessie Hannibal had shed her frou-frou frills and was buttoned to her red ears in a long gray ulster that reached down to her active little feet, now muffled in a pair of galoshes.

The dispute over the bill at an end, the Business Agent fished up a roll from one pocket and a handful of silver and copper coins from the other, counted out the exact amount, waited until the clerk marked a cross against his room number, calling him at seven o'clock A.M., tucked the receipt in his inside pocket, and began the weary ascent.

Steve shook himself free from the chair. This was about his hour. Rising to his legs, he elongated one side of his round body with his pudgy arm, and then the other, yawned sleepily, tipped his hat farther over his eyebrows, called to Larry to be sure and put him down for the 5.40, and mounted the stairs to his room. If he had had any doubts as to the fraudulent character of the whole "shooting match," his chance inspection of the caste had removed them.

On entering his room Steve made several discoveries, no one of which relieved his gloom or sweetened the acidity of his mind.

First, that the temperature was so far below that of a Pullman that the water-pitcher was skimmed with ice and the towel frozen as stiff as a dried codfish. Second, that Jerry, the clown, occupied the room to the right, and the two coryphées the room to the left. Third, that the partitions were thin as paper, or, as Steve expressed it, "thin enough to hear a feller change his mind."

With the turning-off of the gas and the tucking of Steve's fat round face and head under the single blanket and quilt, the sheet gripped about his chin, there came a harsh, rasping cough from the room on his right. Jerry had opened. Steve ducked his head and covered his ears. The clown would stop in a minute, and then Mr. Dodd would drop off to sleep.

Another sound now struck his ear—a woman's voice this time, with a note of sympathy in it. Steve raised his head and listened.

"Say, Jess, ain't that awful? I knew Jerry'd get it on that long jump we made. I ain't heard him cough like that since we left T'ronto."

"Oh, dreadful! And, Molly, he don't say a word 'bout how sick he is. Billy had to help him off with his— Oh, just hear Jerry!"

The talk ceased and Steve snuggled his head again. He wasn't interested in Jerry, or Molly, or Jessie. What he wanted was six hours' sleep, a call at 4.45, and his sample trunk.

Another paroxysm of coughing resounded through the partition, and again Steve freed his ear.

"Jerry ain't got but one little girl left, and she's only five years old. She's up to the Sacred Heart in Montreal. He sends her money every week—he told

55

me so. He showed me her picture oncet. Say! give me some of the cover; it's awful cold, ain't it?"

Steve heard a rustling and tumbling of the bed-clothes as the girls nestled the closer. Molly's voice now broke the short silence.

"Say, Jess, I'm dreadful worried 'bout Jerry. I bet he ain't got no more cover 'n we have. He's right next to us, and 'tain't no warmer where he is than it is here. I'd think he'd tear himself all to pieces with that cough. I hope nothin' 'll happen to him. He ain't like Mathews. Nobody ever heard a cross word out of Jerry, and he'd cut his heart out for ye and——"

Steve covered his head again and shut his eyes. Through the coarse cotton sheet he caught, as he dozed off to sleep (Jerry's cough had now become a familiar sound, and therefore no longer an incentive to insomnia), additional details of Jerry's life, fortunes and misfortunes, in such broken sentences as—

"She never cared for him, so Billy told me. She went off with— Why, sure! didn't you know he got burnt out?—lost his trick ponies when he was with Forepaugh— It'll be awful if we have to leave him behind, and— I'm goin' to see a doctor just as soon as we get to——"

Here Steve fell into oblivion.

Ten minutes later he was startled by the opening of his door. In the dim glow of the hall gas-jet showing through the crack and the transom, his eyes caught the outline of a girl in her night-dress, her hair in two braids down her neck. She was stepping noiselessly and approaching his bed. In her hand she carried a quilt. Bending above him— Steve lying in the shadow she spread the covering gently over his body, tucked the end softly about his throat, and as gently tiptoed out of the room. Then there came a voice from the other side of the partition:

"He ain't coughin' any more—he's asleep. I got it over him. Now get all your clo'es, Molly, and pile 'em on top. We can get along."

Steve lay still. His first impulse was to cry out that they had made a mistake—that Jerry was next door; his next was to slip into Jerry's room and pile the quilt on him. Then he checked himself—the first would alarm and mortify the girls, and the second would be like robbing them of the credit of their generous act. Jerry might wake and the girls would hear, and explanations follow and all the pleasure of their sacrifice be spoiled. No, he'd hand it back to the girls, and say he was much obliged but he didn't need it. Again he stopped—this time with a sudden pull-up. Going into a chorus girl's room, under any pretence whatever, in a hotel at night! No, sir-ee, Bob! Not for Stephen! He had been there; none of that in his!

All this time the quilt was choking him—his breath getting shorter every minute, as if he was being slowly smothered. A peculiar hotness began to creep over the skin of his throat and a small lump to rise near his Adam's apple, followed by a slight moistening of the eyes—all new symptoms to Steve, new since his boyhood.

Suddenly there flashed into his mind the picture of a low-roofed garret room, sheltering a trundle-bed tucked away under the slant of the shingles. In the dim light where he lay he caught the square

58

of the small window, the gaunt limbs of the butter-nut beyond, and could hear, as he listened, the creak of its branches bending in the storm. All about were old-fashioned things—a bureau with brass handles; a spinning-wheel; ropes of onions; a shelf of apples; an old saddle; and a rocking-chair with one arm gone and the bottom half out. A soft tread was heard upon the stairs, a white figure stole in, and a warm hand nestling close to his cheeks tucked the border of a quilt under his chin. Then came a voice. "I thought you might be cold, son."

With a bound Steve sprang from the bed.

For an instant he sat on the edge of the hard mattress, his eyes on the floor, as if in deep thought.

"Those two girls lying there freezing, and all to get that feller warm!" he muttered. "You're a dog, Stephen Dodd—that's what you are—a yellow dog!"

Reaching out noiselessly for his shoes and socks, he drew them toward him, slipped in his feet, dragged on his trousers and shirt, threw his coat around his shoulders—he was beginning to shiver now—opened the door of his room cautiously, let-

ting in more of the glow of the gas-jet, and stole
down the corridor to the staircase. Here he looked
into a black gulf. The only lights were the one by
the clerk's desk and the glow of the stove. Quicken-
ing his steps, he descended the stairs to the lower
floor. The porter would be up, he said to himself, or
the night watchman, or perhaps the clerk; somebody, anyway, would be around. He looked over the
counter, expecting to find Larry in his chair; passed
out to the porter's room and studied the trunks and
boot-stand; peered behind the screen, and finding
no one, made a tour of the floor, opening and
shutting doors. No one was awake.

Then a new thought struck him. This came with
a thumping of one fist in the palm of the other
hand, his face breaking out into a satisfied smile at
his discovery. He remounted the stairs—the first
flight two steps at a time, the second flight one step
at a time, the last few levels on his toes. If he had
intended to burglarize one of the rooms he could
not have been more careful about making a noise.
Entering his own apartment, he picked up the quilt
the girls had spread over him, folded it carefully

and laid it on the floor. Then he stripped off his own blanket and quilt and placed them beside it. These two packages he tucked under his arm, and with the tread of a cat crept down the corridor to the stairway. Once there, he wheeled and with both heels striking the bare floor came tramping toward the girls' room.

Next came a rap like a five-o'clock call—low, so as not to wake the more fortunate in the adjoining rooms, but sure and positive. Steve knew how it sounded.

"Who's there?" cried Molly in a voice that showed that Steve's knuckles had brought her to consciousness. " 'Tain't time to get up, is it?"

"No, I'm the night watchman; some of the folks is complaining of the cold and saying there warn't covering enough, and so I thought you ladies might want some more bedclothes," and Steve squeezed the quilt in through the crack of the door.

"Oh, thank you," began Molly; "we were sort o'——"

"Don't mention it," answered Steve, closing the door tight and shutting off any further remark.

61

The heels were lifted now, and Steve crept to Jerry's door on his toes. For an instant he listened intently until he caught the sound of the labored breathing of the sleeping man, opened the door gently, laid the blanket and quilt he had taken from his own bed over Jerry's emaciated shoulders, and crept out again, dodging into his own room with the same sort of relief in his heart that a sneak thief feels after a successful raid. Here he finished dressing.

Catching up his grip, he moved back his door, peered out to be sure he was not being watched, and tiptoed along the corridor and so on to the floor below.

An hour later the porter, aroused by his alarm clock to get ready for the 5.40, found Steve by the stove. He had dragged up another chair and lay stretched out on the two, his head lost in the upturned collar of his coat, his slouch hat pulled down over his eyes.

"Why, I thought you'd turned in," yawned the porter, dumping a shovelful of coal into the stove.

AN EXTRA BLANKET

"Yes, I did, but I couldn't sleep." There was a note in Steve's voice that made the porter raise his eyes.

"Ain't sick, are ye?"

"No—kind o' nervous—get that way sometimes. Not in your way, am I?"

A MEDAL OF HONOR

A MEDAL OF HONOR

HE was short and thick-set: round-bodied—a bulbous round, like an onion—with alternate layers of waistcoats, two generally, the under one of cotton duck showing a selvage of white, and the outer one of velvet or cloth showing a pattern of dots, stripes, or checks, depending on the prevailing style at the wholesale clothier's where he traded, the whole topped by a sprouting green necktie. Outside this waistcoat drooped a heavy gold chain connecting with a biscuit-shaped watch, the under convex of its lid emblazoned with his monogram in high relief, and the upper concave decorated with a photograph of his best girl.

The face of this inviting and correctly attired young gentleman was likewise round; the ends of the mouth curving upward, not downward—upward, with a continuous smile in each corner, even when the mouth was shut, as if the laugh inside of him were still tickling his funny-bone and the corners of the mouth were recording the vibrations. These uncontrollable movements connected with other hilarious wriggles puckering with merriment under the pupils of his two keen, searching eyes, bright as the lens of a camera and as sensitive and absorbing.

Nothing escaped these eyes—nothing that was worth wasting a plate on. Men and their uses, women and their needs, fellow-travellers with desirable information who were cutting into the bulbous-shaped man's territory, were all focussed by these eyes and deluded by this mouth into giving up their best cash discounts and any other information needed. Some hayseeds might get left, but not Sam Makin.

"Well, I guess not! No flies on Samuel! Up and dressed every minute and 'next' every time!" Such was the universal tribute.

This knowledge did not end with humans. Sam knew the best train out and in, and the best seat in it; the best hotel in town and the best table in the

68

dining-room, as well as the best dish on the bill of fare—not of one town, but of hundreds all over his territory. That is what he paid for, and that was what he intended to have.

When Sam was on the road, in addition to his grip—which held a change of waistcoats (Sam did his finest work with a waistcoat), some collars and a couple of shirts, one to wash and the other to wear, a tooth-brush and a comb—he held the brass checks of four huge trunks made of rawhide and strapped and cornered with iron. These went by weight and were paid for at schedule prices. When a baggage-master overweighed these trunks an ounce and charged accordingly there came an uncomfortable moment and an interchange of opinions, followed by an apology and a deduction, Sam standing by. Only on occasions like these did the smiles disappear from the corners of Sam's mouth.

Whenever these ironclads, however, were elevated to the upper floor of a hotel, and Sam began to make himself at home, the wriggles playing around the corners of his mouth extended quite up his smil-

ing cheeks with the movement of little lizards
darting over a warm stone.

And his own welcome from everybody in the
house was quite as cordial and hilarious.

"Hello, Sam, old man! Number 31's all ready—
mail's on your bureau." This from the clerk.

"Oh! is it you ag'in, Mister Sam? Oh—go 'long
wid ye! Now stop that!" This from the chambermaid.

"It's good to git a look at ye! And them box-cars
o' yourn ain't no bird-cages! Yes, sir—thank ye,
sir." This from the porter.

But it was when the trunks were opened and their
contents spread out on the portable and double-up-
able pine tables, and Bullock & Sons' (of Spring
Falls, Mass.) latest and best assortment of domestic
cutlery was exposed to view, and the room became
crowded with Sam's customers, that the smile on
his face became a veritable coruscation of wriggles
and darts; scurrying around his lips, racing in
circles from his nose to his ears, tumbling over
each other around the corners of his pupils and
beneath the lids; Sam talking all the time, the keen

The room became crowded with Sam's customers.

eyes boring, or taking impressions, the sales increasing every moment.

When the last man was bowed out and the hatches of the ironclads were again shut, anyone could see that Sam had skimmed the cream of the town. The hayseeds might have what was left. Then he would go downstairs, square himself before a long, sloping desk, open a non-stealable inkstand, turn on an electric light, sift out half a dozen sheets of hotel paper, and tell Bullock & Sons all about it.

On this trip Sam's ironclads were not wide open on a hotel table, but tight-locked aboard a Fall River steamer. Sam had a customer in Fall River, good for fifty dozen of B. & S.'s No. 18 scissors, $9 —10 per cent. off and 5 more for cash. The ironclads had been delivered on the boat by the transfer company. Sam had taken a street-car. There was a block, half an hour's delay, and Sam arrived on the string-piece as the gangplank was being hauled aboard.

"Look out, young feller!" said the wharfman; "you're left."

"Look again, you Su-markee!" (nobody knows what Sam means by this epithet), and the drummer threw his leg over the rail of the slowly moving steamer and dropped on her deck as noiselessly as a cat. This done, he lifted a cigar from a bunch stuffed in the outside pocket of the prevailing waist-coat, bit off the end, swept a match along the seam of his "pants" (Sam's own), lit the end of the domestic, blew a ring toward the fast-disappearing wharfman, and turned to get his ticket and state-room, neither of which had he secured.

Just here Mr. Samuel Makin, of Bullock & Sons, manufacturers, etc., etc., received a slight shock.

There was a ticket-office and a clerk, and a rack of state-room keys, just as Sam had expected, but there was also a cue of passengers—a long, winding snake of a cue beginning at the window framing the clerk's face and ending on the upper deck. This crawling line of expectants was of an almost uni-form color, so far as hats were concerned—most of them dark blue and all of them banded about with a gold cord and acorns. The shoulders varied a little, showing a shoulder-strap here and there, and once in a while the top of a medal pinned to a breast pressed tight against some comrade's back. Lower down, whenever the snake parted for an instant, could be seen an armless sleeve and a pair of crutches. As the head of this cue reached the window a key was passed out and the fortunate owner broke away, the coveted prize in his hand, and another expectant took his place.

Sam watched the line for a moment and then turned to a by-stander:

"What's going on here?—a camp-meeting?"

"No. Grand Army of the Republic—going to Boston for two days. Ain't been a berth aboard here for a week. Sofas are going at two dollars, and pillows at seventy-five cents."

Sam's mind reverted for a moment to the look on the wharfman's face, and the corners of his mouth began to play. He edged nearer to the window and caught the clerk's eye.

"No hurry, Billy," and Sam winked, and all the lizards darted out and began racing around the corners of his mouth. " 'Tend to these gents first— I'll call later. Number 15, ain't it?"

The clerk moved the upper lid of his left eye a hair's breadth, took a key from the rack and slipped it under a pile of papers on his desk.

Sam caught the vibration of the lid, tilted his domestic at a higher angle, and went out to view the harbor and the Statue of Liberty and the bridge—any old thing that pleased him. Then this expression slipped from between his lips:

"That was one on the hayseeds! Cold day when you're left, Samuel!"

When supper-time arrived the crowd was so great that checks were issued for two tables, an hour apart. When the captain of the boat and the ranking officer of the G. A. R. filed in, followed by a hungry mob, a lone man was discovered seated at a table nearest the galley where the dishes were hottest and best served. It was Sam. He had come in through the pantry, and the head steward—Sam had known him for years, nearly as long as he had known the clerk—had attended to the other details, one of which was a dish of soft-shell crabs, only enough for half a dozen passengers, and which toothsome viands the head steward scratched off the bill of fare the moment they had been swallowed.

That night Sam sat up on deck until the moon rose over Middle Ground Light, talking shop to another drummer, and then he started for state-room Number 15 with an upper and lower berth (both Sam's), including a set of curtains for each berth—a chair, a washbowl, life-preserver, and swinging light. On his way to this Oriental boudoir he passed through the saloon. It was occupied by a miscellaneous assortment of human beings—men, women and children in all positions of discomfort some sprawled out on the stationary sofas, some flat on the carpet, their backs to the panelling; others nodding on the staircase, determined to sit it out until daylight. On the deck below, close against the woodwork, rolled up in their coats, was here and there a veteran. They had slept that way many a time in the old days with the dull sound of a distant battery lulling them to sleep—they rather liked it.

The next morning, when the crowd swarmed out to board the train at Fall River, Sam tarried a moment at the now deserted ticket-office, smiled blandly at Billy, and laid a greenback on the sill.

"What's the matter, old man, with my holding on to Number 15 till I come back? This boat goes back to New York day after to-morrow, doesn't she?"

Billy nodded, picked up a lead-pencil and put a cross against Number 15; then he handed Sam back his change and the key.

All that day in Fall River Sam sold cutlery, the ironclads doing service. The next day he went to Boston on a later train than the crowd, and had almost a whole car to himself. The third day he returned to Fall River an hour ahead of the special train carrying the Grand Army, and again with half the car to himself. When the special rolled into the depot and was shunted on to the steamboat dock, it looked, in perspective from where Sam stood, like a tenement-house on a hot Sunday—every window and door stuffed with heads, arms, and legs.

Sam studied the mob for a few minutes, felt in his

"pants" pocket for his key, gave it one or two lov-
ing pats with his fingers, and took a turn up the
dock where it was cooler and where the human
avalanche wouldn't run over him.

When the tenement-house was at last unloaded,
it was discovered that it had contained twice as
many people as had filled it two days before. They
had gone to Boston by different lines, and being
now tired out and penniless were returning home
by the cheapest and most comfortable route. They
wanted the salt zephyrs of the sea to fan them
to sleep, and the fish and clams and other marine
delicacies so lavishly served on the Fall River Line
as a tonic for their depleted systems.

Not the eager, expectant crowd that with band
playing and flags flying had swept out of the depot
the day of the advance on Boston! Not that kind
of a crowd at all, but a bedraggled, forlorn,
utterly exhausted and worn-out crowd; children
crying, and pulled along by one arm or hugged to
perspiring breasts; uniforms yellow with dust; men
struggling to keep the surging mass from wives
who had hardly strength left for another step;

flags furled; bass drum with a hole in it; band silent.

Sam looked on and again patted his key. The hayseeds had aired their collars and had "got it in the neck." No G. A. R. for Samuel; no excursions, no celebrations, no picnics for him. He had all his teeth, and an extra wisdom molar for Sundays.

The contents of the tenement now began to press through the closed shed on their way to the gang-plank, and Sam, realizing the size of the mob, and fearing that half of them, including himself, would be left on the dock, slipped into the current and was swept over the temporary bridge, across the deck and up the main staircase leading to the saloon—up to the top step.

Here the current stopped.

Ahead of him was a solid mass, and behind him a pressure that increased every moment and that threatened to push him off his feet. He could get neither forward nor back.

A number of other people were in the same pre-dicament. One was a young woman who, in sheer exhaustion, had seated herself upon the top step

level with the floor of the saloon. Her hair was di-
shevelled, her bonnet awry, her pretty silk cape covered with dust. On her lap lay a boy of five years of
age. Close to her—so close that Sam's shoulder
pressed against his—stood a man in an army hat
with the cord and acorn encircling the crown. On
his breast was pinned a medal. Sam was so close
he could read the inscription: "Fair Oaks," it said,
and then followed the date and the name and number of the regiment. Sam knew what it meant: he
had had an uncle who went to the war, and who
wore a medal. His sword hung over the mantel in
his mother's sitting-room at home. The man before
him had, no doubt, been equally brave: he had saved
the colors the day of the fight, perhaps, or had carried a wounded comrade out of range of a rifle pit,
or had thrown an unexploded shell clear of a tent—
some little thing like that.

Sam had never seen a medal that close before, and
his keen lens absorbed every detail—the ribbon, the
way it was fastened to the cloth, the broad, strong
chest behind it. Then he looked into the man's firm,
determined, kindly face with its piercing black eyes

and closely trimmed mustache, and then over his back and legs. He was wondering now where the ball had struck him, and what particular part of his person had been sacrificed in earning so distinguishing a mark of his country's gratitude.

Then he turned to the woman, and a slight frown gathered on his face when he realized that she alone had blocked his way to the open air and the deck beyond. He could step over any number of men whenever the mass of human beings crushing his ribs and shoulder-blades began once more to move, but a woman—a tired woman—with a boy—out on a jamboree like this, with——

Here Sam stopped, and instinctively felt around among his loose change for his key. Number 15 was all right, any way.

At the touch of the key Sam's face once more resumed its contented look, the lizards darting out to play, as usual.

The boy gave a sharp cry.

The woman put her hand on the child's head, smoothed it softly, and looked up in the face of the man with the medal.

A MEDAL OF HONOR

"And you can get no state-room, George?" she asked in a plaintive tone.

"State-room, Kitty! Why, we couldn't get a pillow. I tried to get a shake-down some'ers, but half these people won't get six feet of space to lie down in, let alone a bed."

"Well, I don't know what we're going to do. Freddie's got a raging fever; I can't hold him here in my arms all night."

Sam shifted his weight to the other foot and concentrated his camera. The man with the medal and the woman with the boy were evidently man and wife. Sam had no little Freddie of his own—no Kitty, in fact—not yet—no home really that he could call his own—never more than a month at a time. A Pullman lower or a third story front in a three-dollar-a-day hotel was often his bed, and a marble-top table with iron legs screwed to the floor of a railroad restaurant and within sound of a big-voiced gateman bawling out the trains, generally his board. Freddie looked like a nice boy, and she looked like a nice woman. Man was O. K., anyhow—didn't give medals of honor to any other

81

kind. Both of them fools, though, or they wouldn't
have brought that kid out——

Again the child turned its head and uttered a
faint cry, this time as if in pain.

Sam freed his arm from the hip bone of the passenger on his left, and said in a sympathetic voice—
unusual for Sam:

"Is this your boy?" The drummer was not a
born conversationalist outside of trade matters, but
he had to begin somewhere.

"Yes, sir." The woman looked up and a flickering smile broke over her lips. "Our only one,
sir."

"Sick, ain't he?"

"Yes, sir; got a high fever."

The man with the medal now wrenched his shoulder loose and turned half round toward Sam. Sam
never looked so jolly nor so trustworthy: the lizards
were in full play all over his cheeks.

"Freddie's all tired out, comrade. I didn't want
to bring him, but Kitty begged so. It was crossing
the Common, in that heat—your company must
have felt it when you come along. The sun beat

down terrible on Freddie—that's what used him up."

Sam felt a glow start somewhere near his heels, struggle up through his spinal column and end in his fingers. Being called "comrade" by a man with a medal on his chest was, somehow, better than being mistaken for a millionaire.

"Can't you get a state-room?" Sam asked. Of course the man couldn't—he had heard him say so. The drummer was merely sparring for time—trying to adjust himself to a new situation—one rare with him. Meanwhile the key of Number 15 was turning in his pocket as uneasily as a grain of corn on a hot shovel.

The man shook his head in a hopeless way. The woman replied in his stead—she, too, had fallen a victim to Sam's smile.

"No, sir, that's the worst of it," she said in a choking voice. "If we only had a pillow we could put Freddie's head on it and I could find some place where he might be comfortable. I don't much mind for myself, but it's dreadful about Freddie—" and she bent her head over the child.

Sam thought of the upper berth in Number 15 with two pillows and the lower berth with two more. By this time the key of Number 15 had reached a white heat.

"Well, I guess I can help out," Sam blurted. "I've got a state-room—got two berths in it. Just suit you, come to think of it. Here"— and he dragged out the key—"Number 15—main deck—you can't miss it. Put the kid there and bunk in yourselves—" and he dropped the key in the woman's lap, his voice quivering, a lump in his throat the size of a hen's egg.

"Oh, sir, we couldn't!" cried the woman.

"No, comrade," interrupted the man, "we can't do that; we——"

Sam heard, but he did not tarry. With one of his nimble springs he lunged through the crowd, his big fat shoulders breasting the mob, wormed himself out into the air; slipped down a ladder to the deck below, interviewed the steward, borrowed a blanket and a pillow and proceeded to hunt up the ironclads. If the worst came to the worst he would string them in a row, spread his blanket on top and roll up for the night. Their height would keep him off the deck, and the roof above them would protect him from the weather should a squall come up.

This done, he drew out a domestic from the upper pocket, bit off the end, slid a match along the well-worn seam and blew a ring out to sea.

"Couldn't let that kid sit up all night, you know," he muttered to himself. "Not your Uncle Joseph: no sir-ee—" and he wedged his way back to the deck again.

An hour later, with his blanket over his shoulder and his pillow under his arm, Sam again sought his ironclads. Steward, chief cook, clerk—everything had failed. The trunks with the pillow and blanket were all that was left.

It was after nine o'clock now, and the summer twilight had faded and only the steamer's lanterns shone on the heads of the people. As he passed the companion-way he ran into a man in an army hat. Backing away in apology he caught the glint of a medal. Then came a familiar voice:

"Comrade, where you been keeping yourself? I've been hunting you all over the boat. You're the man gave me the key, ain't you?"

"*Sure!* How's the kid? Is he all right? Didn't I tell you you'd find that up-to-date? It's a cracker-jack, that room is; I've had it before. Tell me, how's the kid and the wife—kind o' comfy, ain't they?"

"Both are all right. Freddie's in the lower berth and Kitty sitting by him. He's asleep, and the fever's going down; ain't near so hot as he was. You're white, comrade, all the way through." The man's big hand closed over Sam's in a warm embrace. "I thank you for it. You did us a good turn and we ain't going to forget you."

Sam kept edging away; what hurt him most was being thanked.

"But that ain't what I've been hunting you for, comrade," the man continued. "You didn't get a state-room, did you?"

"No," said Sam, shaking his head and still backing away. "But I'm all right—got a pillow and a blanket—see!" and he held them up. "You needn't worry, old man. This ain't nothing to the way I sleep sometimes. I'm one of those fellows can bunk in anywhere." Sam was now in sight of his trunks.

"Yes," answered the man, still keeping close to Sam, "that's just what we thought would happen; that's what *does* worry us, and worry us bad. You ain't going to bunk in anywhere—not by a blamed sight! Kitty and I have been talking it over, and what Kitty says goes! There's two bunks in that state-room; Kitty's in one 'longside of the boy, and you got to sleep in the other."

"Me!—well—but—why, man!" Sam's astonishment took his breath away.

" You got to!" The man meant it.

"But I won't!" said Sam in a determined voice.

"Well, then, out goes Kitty and the boy! You think I'm going to sleep in your bunk, and have you stretched out here on a plank some'ers! No, sir! You *got* to, I tell you!"

"Why, see here!" Sam was floundering about now as helplessly as if he had been thrown overboard with his hands tied.

"There ain't no seeing about it, comrade." The

man was close to him now, his eyes boring into Sam's with a look in them as if he was taking aim.

"You say I've got to get into the upper berth?" asked Sam in a baffled tone.

"Yes."

Sam ruminated: "When?"

"When Kitty gets to bed."

"How'll I know?"

"I'll come for you."

"All right—you'll find me here."

Then Sam turned up the deck muttering to himself: "That's one on you, Sam-u-e-l—one under the chin-whisker. Got to—eh? Well, for the love of Mike!"

In ten minutes Sam heard a whistle and raised his head. The man with the medal was leaning over the rail looking down at him.

Sam mounted the steps and picked his way among the passengers sprawled over the floor and deck. The man advanced to meet him, smiled contentedly, walked along the corridor, put his hand on the knob of the door of Number 15, opened it noiselessly, beckoned silently, waited until Sam had stepped over the threshold and closed the door upon him. Then the man tiptoed back to the saloon.

Sam looked about him. The curtains of the lower berth were drawn; the curtains of the upper one were wide open. On a chair was his bag, and on a hook by the shuttered window the cape and hat of the wife and the clothes of the sleeping boy.

At the sight of the wee jacket and little half-breeches, tiny socks and cap, Sam stopped short. He had never before slept in a room with a child, and a strange feeling, amounting almost to awe, crept over him. It was as if he had stepped suddenly into a shrine and had been confronted by the altar. The low-turned lamp and the silence—no sound came from either of the occupants—only added to the force of the impression.

Sam slipped off his coat and shoes, hung the first on a peg and laid the others on the floor; loosened his collar, mounted the chair, drew himself stealthily into the upper berth; closed the curtains and stretched himself out. As his head touched the pillow a soft, gentle, rested voice said:

"I can't tell you how grateful we are, sir—goodnight."

"Don't mention it, ma'am," whispered Sam in answer; "mighty nice of you to let me come," and he dropped off to sleep.

At the breaking of the dawn Sam woke with a start; ran his eye around the room until he found his bearings; drew his legs together from the coverlet; let himself down as stealthily as a cat walking over teacups; picked up his shoes, slipped his arms into his coat, gave a glance at the closed curtains sheltering the mother and child, and crossed the room on his way to the door with the tread of a burglar.

Reaching out his hand in the dim light he studied the lock for an instant, settled in his mind which knob to turn so as to make the least noise, and swung back the door.

Outside on the mat, sound asleep, so close that he almost stepped on him, lay the Man with the Medal.

THE RAJAH OF BUNGPORE

THE RAJAH OF BUNGPORE

IT was the crush hour at Sherry's. A steady
stream of men and women in smart toilettes—the
smartest the town afforded—had flowed in under
the street awning, through the doorway guarded
by flunkeys, past the dressing-rooms and coat-
racks, and were now banked up in the spacious hall
waiting for tables, the men standing about, the
women resting on the chairs and divans listening to
the music of the Hungarian band or chatting with
one another. The two cafés were full—had been
since seven o'clock, every table being occupied except two. One of these had been reserved that morning by my dear friend Marny, the distinguished
painter of portraits—I being his guest—and the
other, so the head-waiter told us, awaited the arrival of Mr. John Stirling, who would entertain a
party of six.

93

AT CLOSE RANGE

When Marny was a poor devil of an illustrator, and worked for the funny column of the weekly papers—we had studios in the same building—we used to dine at Porcelli's, the price of the two meals equalling the value of one American trade dollar, and including one bottle of vin ordinaire. Now that Marny wears a ribbon in his button-hole, has a suite of rooms that look like a museum, man-servants and maid-servants, including an English butler whose principal business is to see that Marny is not disturbed, a line of carriages before his door on his reception days, and refuses two portraits a week at his own prices—we sometimes dine at Sherry's.

As I am still a staid old landscape painter living up three flights of stairs with no one to wait on me but myself and the ten-year-old daughter of the janitor, I must admit that these occasional forays into the whirl of fashionable life afford me not only infinite enjoyment, but add greatly to my knowledge of human nature.

As we followed the waiter into the café, a group of half a dozen men, all in full dress, emerged from a side room and preceded us into the restaurant, led

94

by a handsome young fellow of thirty. The next
moment they grouped themselves about the other
reserved table, the young fellow seating his guests
himself, drawing out each chair with some remark
that kept the whole party laughing.

When we had settled into our own chairs, and
my host had spread his napkin and looked about
him, the young fellow nodded his head at Marny,
clasped his two hands together, shook them together
heartily, and followed this substitute for a closer
welcome by kissing his hand at him.

Marny returned the courtesy by a similar handshake, and bending his head said in a low voice,
"The Rajah must be in luck to-night."

"Who?" I asked. My acquaintance with foreign
potentates is necessarily limited.

"The Rajah—Jack Stirling. Take a look at him.
You'll never see his match; nobody has yet."

I shifted my chair a little, turned my head in the
opposite direction, and then slowly covering Stirling with my gaze—the polite way of staring at a
stranger—got a full view of the man's face and
figure; rather a difficult thing on a crowded night

at Sherry's, unless the tables are close together. What I saw was a well-built, athletic-looking young man with a smooth-shaven face, laughing eyes, a Cupid mouth, curly brown hair, and a fresh ruddy complexion; a Lord Byron sort of a young fellow with a modern up-to-date training. He was evidently charming his guests, for every man's head was bent forward seemingly hanging on each word that fell from his lips.

"A rajah, is he? He don't look like an Oriental."

"He isn't. He was born in New Jersey."

"Is he an artist?"

"Yes, five or six different kinds; he draws better than I do; plays on three instruments, and speaks five languages."

"Rich?"

"No—dead broke half the time."

I glanced at the young fellow's faultless appearance and the group of men he was entertaining. My eye took in the array of bottles, the number of wineglasses of various sizes, and the mass of roses that decorated the centre of the table. Such appointments and accompaniments are not generally

96

the property of the poor. Then, again, I remembered we were at Sherry's.

"What does he do for a living, then?" I asked.

"Do for a living? He doesn't do anything for a living. He's a purveyor of cheerfulness. He wakes up every morning with a fresh stock of happiness, more than he can use himself, and he trades it off during the day for anything he can get."

"What kind of things?" I was a little hazy over Marny's meaning.

"Oh, dinners—social, of course—board bills, tailor's bills, invitations to country houses, voyages on yachts—anything that comes along and of which he may be in need at the time. Most interesting man in town. Everybody loves him. Known all over the world. If a fellow gets sick, Stirling waltzes in, fires out the nurse, puts on a linen duster, starts an alcohol lamp for gruel, and never leaves till you are out again. All the time he is pumping laughs into you and bracing you up so that you get well twice as quick. Did it for me once for five weeks on a stretch, when I was laid up in my studio with inflammatory rheumatism, with my grub bills hung

97

up in the restaurant downstairs, and my rent three months overdue. Fed me on the fat of the land, too. Soup from Delmonico's, birds from some swell house up the Avenue, where he had been dining—sent that same night with the compliments of his hostess with a 'Please forgive me, but dear Mr. Stirling tells me how ill you have been, and at his suggestion, and with every sympathy for your sufferings— please accept.' Oh, I tell you he's a daisy!"

Here a laugh sounded from Stirling's table.

"Who's he got in tow now?" I asked, as my eyes roamed over the merry party.

"That fat fellow in eyeglasses is Crofield the banker, and the hatchet-faced man with white whiskers is John Riggs from Denver, President of the C. A.—worth ten millions. I don't know the others — some bored-to-death fellows, perhaps, starving for a laugh. Jack ought to go slow, for he's dead broke—told me so yesterday."

"Perhaps Riggs is paying for the dinner." This was an impertinent suggestion, I know; but then sometimes I can be impertinent—especially when some of my pet theories have to be defended.

THE RAJAH OF BUNGPORE

"Not if Jack invited him. He's the last man in
the world to sponge on anybody. Inviting a man to
dinner and leaving his pocketbook in his other coat
is not Jack's way. If he hasn't got the money in
his own clothes, he'll find it somehow, but not in
their clothes."

"Well, but at times he *must* have ready money,"
I insisted. "He can't be living on credit all the
time." I have had to work for all my pennies, am
of a practical turn of mind, and often live in con-
stant dread of the first of every month—that fatal
pay-day from which there is no escape. The success,
therefore, of another fellow along different and
more luxurious lines naturally irritates me.

"Yes, now and then he does need money. But
that never bothers Jack. When his tailor, or his
shoemaker, or his landlord gets him into a corner,
he sends the bill to some of his friends to pay for
him. They never come back—anybody would do
Stirling a favor, and they know that he never calls
on them unless he is up against it solid."

I instinctively ran over in my mind which of my
own friends I would approach, in a similar emer-

99

gency, and the notes I would receive in reply. Stirling must know rather a stupid lot of men or they couldn't be buncoed so easily, I thought.

Soup was now being served, and Marny and the waiter were discussing the merits of certain vintages, my host insisting on a bottle of '84 in place of the '82, then in the waiter's hand.

During the episode I had the opportunity to study Stirling's table. I noticed that hardly a man entered the room who did not stop and lay his hand affectionately on Stirling's shoulder, bending over and joining in the laugh. His guests, too—those about his table—seemed equally loyal and happy. Riggs's hard business face—evidently a man of serious life—was beaming with merriment and twice as wide, under Jack's leadership, and Crofield and the others were leaning forward, their eyes fixed on their host, waiting for the point of his story, then breaking out together in a simultaneous laugh that could be heard all over our part of the room.

When Marny had received the wine he wanted —it's extraordinary how critical a man's palate becomes when his income is thousands a year instead of dollars—I opened up again with my battery of questions. His friend had upset all my formulas and made a laughing-stock of my most precious traditions. "Pay as you go and keep out of debt" seemed to belong to a past age.

"Speaking of your friend, the Rajah, as you call him," I asked, "and his making his friends pay his bills—does he ever pay back?"

"Always, when he gets it."

"Well, where *does* he get it—cards?" It seemed to me now that I saw some comforting light ahead, dense as I am at times.

"Cards! Not much—never played a game in his life. Not that kind of a man."

"How, then?" I wanted the facts. There must be some way in which a man like Stirling could live, keep out of jail, and keep his friends—friends like Marny.

"Same way. Just chucks around cheerfulness to everybody who wants it, and 'most everybody does. As to ready money, there's hardly one of his rich friends in the Street who hasn't a Jack Stirling account on his books. And they are always lucky, for what they buy for Jack Stirling is sure to go up. Got to be a superstition, really. I know one broker who sent him over three thousand dollars last fall—made it for him out of a rise in some coal stock. Wrote him a note and told him he still had two thousand dollars to his credit on his books, which he would hold as a stake to make another turn on next time he saw a sure thing in sight. I was with Jack when he opened the letter. What do you think he did? He pulled out his bureau drawer, found a slip of paper containing a list of his debts, sat down and wrote out a check for each one of his creditors and enclosed them in the most charming little notes with marginal sketches—some in water-color—which every man of them preserves now as souvenirs. I've got one framed in my studio—regular little Fortuny—and the check is framed in with it. Never cashed it and never will. The Rajah, I tell you, old man, is very punctilious about his debts, no matter how small they are. Gave me fifteen shillings last time I went to Cairo to pay some duffer that lived up a street back of Shepheard's, a red-faced Englishman who had helped Jack out of a hole the year before, and who would have pensioned the Rajah for life if he could have induced him to pass the rest of his years with him. And he only saw him for two days! That's the funny thing about Jack. He never forgets his creditors, and his creditors never forget him. I'll tell you about this old Cairo lobster—that's what he looked like—red and claw-y.

"When I found him he was stretched in a chair trying to cool off; he didn't even have the decency to get on his feet.

" 'Who?' he snapped out. Just as if I had been a book agent.

" 'Mr. John Stirling of New York.'

" 'Owes *me* fifteen shillings?'

" 'That's what he said, and here it is,' and I handed him the silver.

" 'Young man,' he says, glowering at me, 'I don't know what your game is, but I'll tell you right here you can't play it on me. Never heard of *Mister*-John-Stirling-of-New-York in my life. So you can put your money back.' I wasn't going to be whipped by the old shell-fish, and then I didn't

103

like the way he spoke of Jack. I knew he was the right man, for Jack doesn't make mistakes—not about things like that. So I went at him on another tack.

" 'Weren't you up at Philæ two years ago in a dahabieh?'

" 'Yes.'

" 'And didn't you meet four or five young Americans who came up on the steamer, and who got into a scrape over their fare?'

" 'I might—I can't recollect everybody I meet— don't want to—half of 'em—' All this time I was standing, remember.

" 'And didn't you—' I was going on to say, but he jumped from his chair and was fumbling about a bookcase.

" 'Ah, here it is!' he cried out. 'Here's a book of photographs of a whole raft of young fellows I met up the Nile on that trip. Most of 'em owed me something and still do. Pick out the man now you say owes me fifteen shillings and wants to pay it.'

" 'There he is—one of those three.'

"The old fellow adjusted his glasses.

THE RAJAH OF BUNGPORE

" 'The Rajah! That man! Know him? Best lad
I ever met in my life. I'm damned if I take his
money, and you can go home and tell him so.' He
did, though, and I sat with him until three o'clock
in the morning talking about Jack, and I had all
I could do getting away from him then. Wanted me
to move in next day bag and baggage, and stay a
month with him. He wasn't so bad when I came to
know him, if he was red and claw-y."

I again devoted my thoughts to the dinner—
what I could spare from the remarkable personage
Marny had been discussing, and who still sat within
a few tables of us. My friend's story had opened
up a new view of life, one that I had never expected
to see personified in any one man. The old-fashioned
rules by which I had been brought up—the rules
of "An eye for an eye," and "Earn thy bread by
the sweat of thy brow," etc.—seemed to have lost
their meaning. The Rajah's method, it seemed to
me, if persisted in, might help solve the new problem of the day—"the joy of living"—always a
colossal joke with me. I determined to know something more of this lazy apostle in a dress suit who

dispensed sweetness and light at some other fellow's expense.

"Why do you call him 'The Rajah,' Marny?" I asked.

"Oh, he got that in India. A lot of people like that old lobster in Cairo don't know him by any other name."

"What did he do in India?"

"Nothing in particular—just kept on being himself—just as he does everywhere."

"Tell me about it."

"Well, I got it from Ashburton, a member of the Alpine Club in London. But everybody knows the story—wonder you haven't heard it. You ought to come out of your hole, old man, and see what's going on in the world. You live up in that den of yours, and the procession goes by and you don't even hear the band. You ought to know Jack— he'd do you a lot of good," and Marny looked at me curiously—as a physician would, who, when he prescribes for you, tells you only one-half of your ailment.

I did not interrupt my friend—I wasn't getting

thousands for a child's head, and twice that price for the mother in green silk and diamonds. And I couldn't afford to hang out my window and watch any kind of procession, figurative or otherwise. Nor could I afford to exchange dinners with John Stirling.

"Do you want me to tell you about that time the Rajah had in India? Well, move your glass this way," and my host picked up the '84. "Ashburton," continued Marny, and he filled my glass to the brim, "is one of those globe-trotters who does mountain-tops for exercise. He knows the Andes as well as he does the glaciers in Switzerland; has been up the Matterhorn and Mont Blanc, and every other snow-capped peak within reach, and so he thought he'd try the Himalayas. You know how these Englishmen are—the rich ones. At twenty-five a good many of them have exhausted life. Some shoot tigers, some fit out caravans and cross deserts, some get lost in African jungles, and some come here and go out West for big game; anything that will keep them from being bored to death before they are thirty-five years of age. Ashburton was that kind.

107

"He had only been home ten days—he had spent two years in Yucatan looking up Toltec ruins—when this Himalaya trip got into his head. Question was, whom could he get to go with him, for these fellows hate to be alone. Some of the men he wanted hadn't returned from their own wild-goose chases; others couldn't get away—one was running for Parliament, I think—and so Ashburton, cursing his luck, had about made up his mind to try it alone, when he ran across Jack one day in the club.

" 'Hello, Stirling! Thought you'd sailed for America.'

" 'No,' said Jack, 'I go next week. What are you doing here? Thought you had gone to India.'

" 'Can't get anybody to go with me,' answered Ashburton.

" 'Where do you go first?'

" 'To Calcutta by steamer, and then strike in and up to the foot-hills.'

" 'For how long?'

" 'About a year. Come with me like a decent man.'

" 'Can't. Only got money enough to get home, and I don't like climbing.'

" 'Money hasn't got anything to do with it—you go as my guest. As to climbing, you won't have to climb an inch. I'll leave you at the foot-hills in a bungalow, with somebody to take care of you, and you can stay there until I come back.'

" 'How long will you be climbing?'

" 'About two months.'

" 'When do you start?'

" 'To-morrow, at daylight.'

" 'All right, I'll be on board.'

"Going out, Jack got up charades and all sorts of performances; rescued a man overboard, striking the water about as soon as the man did, and holding on to him until the lifeboat reached them; studied navigation and took observations every day until he learned how; started a school for the children—there were a dozen on board—and told them fairy tales by the hour; and by the time the steamer reached Calcutta every man, woman, and child had fallen in love with him. One old Maharajah, who was on board, took such a fancy to him that he insisted

109

on Jack's spending a year with him, and there came near being a precious row when he refused, which of course he had to do, being Ashburton's guest.

"When the two got to where Jack was to camp out and wait for Ashburton's return from his climb —it was a little spot called Bungpore—the Englishman fitted up a place just as he said he would; left two men to look after him—one to cook and the other to wait on him—fell on Jack's neck, for he hated the worst kind to leave him, and disappeared into the brush with his retainers—or whatever he did disappear into and with—I never climbed the Himalayas, and so I'm a little hazy over these details. And that's the last Ashburton saw of Jack until he returned two months later."

Marny emptied his glass, flicked the ashes from his cigarette, beckoned to the waiter, and gave him an order for a second bottle of '84. During the break in the story I made another critical examination of the hero, as he sat surrounded by his guests, his face beaming, the light falling on his immaculate shirt-front. I noted the size of his arm and the depth of his chest, and his lithe, muscular

110

thighs. I noticed, too, how quickly he gained his feet when welcoming a friend, who had just stopped at his table. I understood now how the drowning sailor came to be saved.

The wine matter settled, Marny took some fresh cigarettes from his silver case, passed one to me, and held a match to both in turn. Between the puffs I again brought the talk back to the man who now interested me intensely. I was afraid we would be interrupted and I have to wait before finding out why his friend was called the "Rajah."

"I should think he would have gone with him instead of staying behind and living off his bounty," I ventured.

"Yes—I know you would, old man, but Jack thought differently, not being built along your lines. You've got to know him—I tell you, he'll do you a lot of good. Stirling saw that, if he went, it would only double Ashburton's expense account, and so he squatted down to wait with just money enough to get along those two months, and not another cent. Told Ashburton he wanted to learn Hindustanee, and he couldn't do it if he was sliding

111

down glaciers and getting his feet wet—it would keep him from studying."

"And was Stirling waiting for him when Ashburton came back?'"

"Waiting for him! Well, I guess! First thing Ashburton ran up against was one of the blackamoors he had hired to take care of Jack. When he had left the fellow he was clothed in a full suit of yellow dust with a rag around his loins. Now he was gotten up in a red turban and pajamas trimmed with gewgaws. The blackamoor prostrated himself and began kotowing backward toward a marquee erected on a little knoll under some trees and surrounded by elephants in gorgeous trappings. 'The Rajah of Bungpore'—that was Jack—'had sent him,' he said, 'to conduct his Royal Highness into the presence of his illustrious master!'

"When Ashburton reached the door of the marquee and peered in, he saw Jack lying back on an Oriental couch at the other end smoking the pipe of the country—whatever that was—and surrounded by a collection of Hottentots of various

112

At his feet knelt two Hindu merchants displaying their wares.

sizes and colors, who fell on their foreheads every
time Jack crooked his finger. At his feet knelt two
Hindoo merchants displaying their wares—pearls,
ivories, precious stones, arms, porcelains—stuffs
of a quality and price, Ashburton told me, that took
his breath away. Jack kept on—he made out he
didn't see Ashburton—his slaves bearing the pur-
chases away and depositing them on a low inlaid
table—teakwood, I guess—in one corner of the
marquee, while a confidential Lord of the Treasury
took the coin of the realm from a bag or gourd—
or whatever he did take it from—and paid the shot.

"When the audience was over, Jack waved everybody outside with a commanding gesture, and still
lolling on his rugs—or maybe his tiger skins—told
his Grand Vizier to conduct the strange man to his
august presence. Then Jack rose from this throne,
dismissed the Grand Vizier, and fell into Ashburton's arms roaring with laughter."

"And Ashburton had to foot the bills, I suppose," I blurted out. It is astonishing how suspi-
cious and mean a man gets sometimes who mixes
as little as I do with what Marny calls "the swim."

"Ashburton foot the bills! Not much! Listen, you six by nine! Stirling hadn't been alone more than a week when along comes the Maharajah he had met on the steamer. He lived up in that part of the country, and one of his private detectives had told him that somebody was camping out on his lot. Down he came in a white heat, with a bag of bow-strings and a squad of the 'Finest' in pink trousers and spears. I get these details all wrong, old man —they might have been in frock-coats for all I know or care—but what I'm after is the Oriental atmosphere—a sort of property background with my principal figure high up on the canvas—and one costume is as good as another.

"When the old Maharajah found out it was Jack instead of some squatter, he fell all over himself with joy. Wanted to take him up to his marble palace, open up everything, unlock a harem, trot out a half-dozen chorus girls in bangles and mosquito-net bloomers, and do a lot of comfortable things for him. But Jack said No. He was put here to stay, and here he was going to stay if he had to call out every man in his army. The old fellow saw the joke and said all right, here he *should* stay; and before night he had moved down a tent, and a body-guard, and an elephant or two for local color, so as to make it real Oriental for Jack, and the next day he sent him down a bag of gold, and servants, and a cook. Every pedler who appeared after that he passed along to Jack, and before Ashburton turned up Stirling had a collection of curios worth a fortune. One-half of them he gave to Ashburton and the other half be brought home to his friends. That inlaid elephant's tusk hanging up in my studio is one of them—you remember it."

As Marny finished, one of the waiters who had been serving Stirling and his guests approached our table under the direction of the Rajah's finger, and, bending over Marny, whispered something in his ear. He had the cashier's slip in his hand and Stirling's visiting card.

Marny laid the bill beside his plate, glanced at the card with a laugh, his face lighting up, and then passed it to me. It read as follows: "Not a red and no credit. Sign it for Jack."

Marny raised his eyes, nodded his head at Stirling, kissed his finger-tips at him, fished up his gold chain, slid out a pencil dangling at its end, wrote his name across the slip, and said in a whisper to the waiter: "Take this to the manager and have him charge it to my account."

When we had finished our dinner and were passing out abreast of Stirling's table, the Rajah rose to his feet, his guests all standing about him, their glasses in their hands—Riggs's whiskers stood straight, he was so happy—and, waving his own glass toward my host, said: "Gentlemen, I give you Marny, the Master, the Velasquez of modern times!"

.   .   .   .

Some weeks later I called at Marny's studio. He was out. On the easel stood a full-length portrait of Riggs, the millionaire, his thin, hatchet-shaped face and white whiskers in high relief against a dark background. Scattered about the room were smaller heads bearing a strong resemblance to the great president. Jack had evidently corralled the entire family—and all out of that dinner at Sherry's.

116

THE RAJAH OF BUNGPORE

I shut the door of Marny's studio softly behind
me, tiptoed downstairs, dropped into a restaurant
under the sidewalk, and dined alone.

Marny is right. The only way to hear the band
is to keep up with the procession.

My philosophy is a failure.

THE SOLDO OF THE
CASTELLANI

THE SOLDO OF THE CASTELLANI

THE Via Garibaldi is astir to-day. From the Ponte Veneta Marina, next the caffè of the same name—it is but a step—to the big iron gates of the Public Gardens, is a moving throng of Venetians, their chatter filling the soft September air. Flags are waving—all kinds of flags, and of all colors; gay lanterns of quaint patterns are festooned from window to window; old velvets and rare stuffs, some in rags and tatters, so often have they been used, stream out from the balconies crowded with pretty Venetians shading their faces with their parasols as they watch the crowds below. In and out of this mass of holiday-makers move the pedlers crying their wares, some selling figs, their scales of polished brass jingling as they walk; some with gay handkerchiefs and

121

scarfs draped about their trays; here and there one stands beside a tripod holding a big earthen dish filled with *fulpi*—miniature devil-fish about as big as a toad—so ugly that no man, however hungry, except, perhaps, a Venetian, dares swallow one with his eyes open.

Along this stretch of waving flags, gay-colored lanterns, and joyous people, are two places where the throngs are thickest. One is the Caffè Veneta Marina, its door within a cigarette's toss of the first step of the curving bridge of the same name, and the other is the Caffè Beneto, a smaller caffè farther down the wide street—wide for Venice. The Caffè Veneta Marina contains but a single room level with the street, and on gala days its tables and chairs are pushed quite out upon the marble flags. The Caffè Beneto runs through to the waters of the Grand Canal and opens on a veranda fitted with a short flight of steps at which the gondolas often land their passengers.

These two caffès are the headquarters of two opposing factions of gondoliers, enemies for centuries, since the founding of their guild, in fact

—the Nicolletti, whose caps in the old days were black, and the Castellani, whose caps were red. The first were publicans, renowned for their prowess with the oar, but rough and outspoken, boastful in victory, bitter in defeat. The second were aristocrats, serving the Doge and often of great service to the State—men distinguished for their courtesy as well as for their courage. These attributes have followed these two guilds down to the present day.

Every year when the leaves of the sycamores in the Public Gardens fade into brown gold, and the great dome of the Salute, glistening like a huge pink pearl, looms above the soft September haze that blurs the water line, these two guilds—the Nicolletti and Castellani—meet in combat, each producing its best oarsmen.

To-day the course is from the wall of the Public Gardens to the Lido and back. Young Francesco Portera, the idol of the shipyards, a big-boned Venetian, short-armed and strong, is to row for the Nicolletti, and Luigi Zanaletto, a man near twice his age, for the Castellani.

AT CLOSE RANGE

For days there has been no other talk than this gondola race. Never in any September has the betting run so high. So great is the interest in the contest that every morning for a week the line of people at the Monte di Pietà—the Government pawn shop—has extended out into the great corridor of the Palazzo, every arm and pocket filled with clothing, jewels, knick-knacks, everything the owners can and cannot spare, to be pawned in exchange for the money needed to bet on this race.

There is good cause for this unusual excitement. While Luigi is known as the successful winner of the four annual races preceding this one, carrying the flag of the Castellani to victory against all comers, and each year a new contestant, many of his enemies insist that the pace has told on him; that despite his great reach of arm and sinewy legs, his strength, by reason of his age—they are all old at forty in Venice (except the Castellani)—is failing, and that for him to win this fifth and last race would be more than any guild could expect, glorious as would be the result. Others, more knowing, argued that while Francesco had an arm like a blacksmith and could strike a blow that would fell an ox, he lacked that refinement of training which made the ideal oarsman; that it was not so much the size or quality of the muscles as it was the man who used them; that blood and brains were more than brute force.

Still another feature added zest and interest to the race, especially to members of the opposing guilds. There was an unwritten law of Venice that no man of either guild could win more than five races in succession—a foolish law, many thought, for no oarsman had accomplished it. This done, the victor retired on his laurels. Ever after he became *Primo*—the envied of his craft, the well-beloved of all the women of his quarter, young and old alike. Should Luigi Zanaletto win this fifth race, no Nicolletti could show their faces for very shame on the Piazza. For weeks thereafter they would be made the butt of the good-natured badinage of the populace. If, however, Luigi should lose this fifth and last race, the spell would be broken and some champion of the Nicolletti—perhaps this very

Francesco, with the initiative of this race, might gain succeeding victories and so the Nicolletti regain the ground they had lost through Luigi's former prowess.

Those of his guild, however, those who knew and loved Luigi, had no such misgivings as to the outcome. They lost no sleep over his expected defeat. As their champion stepped from his gondola this beautiful September morning, laying his oar along its side, and mounted the marble steps of the landing opposite the Caffè Veneta Marina, those who got close enough to note his superb condition only added to their wagers. Six feet and an inch, straight, with willowy arms strengthened by steel cords tied in knots above the elbows, hauled taut along the wrists and anchored in the hands—grips of steel, these hands, with thumbs and forefingers strong as the jaws of a vice (he wields and guides his oar with these); waist like a woman's, the ribs outlined through the cross-barred boating shirt; back and stomach in-curved, laced and clamped by a red sash; thighs and calves of lapped leather; shoulders a beam of wood—square, hard, unyield-

ing; neck an upward sweep tanned to a ruddy
brown, ending in a mass of black hair, curly as a
dog's and as strong and glistening.

And his face! Stop some morning before the
church of Santi Giovanni e Paolo, and look up into
the face of the great Colleoni as he sits bestride
his bronze horse, and ask the noble soldier to doff
his helmet. Then follow the firm lines of the mouth,
the wide brow, strong nose, and iron chin. Add to
this a skin bronzed to copper by the sun, a pair of
laughing eyes, and an out-pointed mustache, and
you have Luigi.

And the air of the man! Only gondoliers, of all
serving-men, have this humble fearlessness of manner—a manner which combines the dignity of the
patrician with the humility of the servant. It is
their calling which marks the difference. Small as
is the gondola among all water craft, the gondolier
is yet its master, free to come and free to go. The
wide stretch of the sea is his—not another's: a
sea hemmed about by the palaces of ancestors who
for ten centuries dominated the globe.

.   .   .   .

But Luigi is still standing on the marble steps of the landing opposite the Caffè Veneta Marina this lovely September day, doffing his cap to the admiring throng, just as Colleoni would have doffed his, and with equal grace. Not the red cap of his guild—that has been laid aside for two centuries—but his wide straw hat, with his colors wound about it.

As he made his way slowly through the crowd toward the caffè, an old woman who had been waiting for him—wrinkled, gray-haired, a black shawl about her head held tight to the chin by her skinny fingers, her eyes peering from its folds —stepped in front of him. She lived near his home and was godmother to one of his children.

"Luigi Zanaletto!" she cried, catching him by the wrist.

"Yes, good mother."

"That idiot Marco told my Amalia last night that you will lose the race. He has been to the Pietà and will bet all his money on Francesco."

"And why not, good mother? Why do you worry?"

"Because the two fools will have no money to be married on. They are called in San Rosario next Sunday, and the next is their wedding-day. He has pawned the boat his uncle gave him."

"And if he wins?"

"He will not win, Luigi. When that brute came in from the little race we had last week I was passing in a sandolo on my way to San Giorgio. He was panting like a child after a run. If he had no breath left in him then, where will he be to-day?"

"One cannot tell, good mother. Who told the boy I would lose the race?"

"Beppo Cavalli."

"Ah! the Nicolletti," muttered Luigi.

"Yes."

"He has a boy, too, has he not, good mother?"

"Yes, Amalia loved him once; now she loves Marco. These girls are like the wind, Luigi. They never blow two days alike."

Luigi stopped and looked out toward the lagoon. He knew Cavalli. In summer he rowed a barca; in winter he kept a wine shop and sold

129

untaxed salt and smuggled cigarettes to his customers. The crowd pressed closer, listening.

"Beppo Cavalli, good mother," he said, slowly, "means ill to the boy Marco and to your daughter. The Cavallis are not backing Francesco. They talk loud, but there is not a soldo for him among them. Cavalli would get that girl for his son; she is pretty and would bring customers to his shop. Where is Marco?"

"He is at the Caffè Beneto with Cavalli and Francesco. I have tired my tongue out talking to Marco, and so has Amalia. His head is fixed like a stone. Francesco is getting ready for this afternoon, but it will do him no good. He has not arms like this. Is it not so, men?"—and she lifted Luigi's arm and held it up that the crowd might see.

A great cheer went up in answer, and was echoed by the crowd about the caffè door. Luigi among the people of his quarter was like their religion.

The champion had now reached one of the tables of the caffè. Drawing out a chair, he bent forward, shook hands with old Guido, the proprietor, crooked his fingers gallantly at a group of women in an overhanging balcony, and was just taking his seat when a young girl edged her way through the circle and slipped her arm around the woman's neck. She had the low brow surmounted by masses of jet-black hair, drooping, sleepy eyelids shading slumbering, passionate eyes, sensitive sweet mouth and oval face common to her class. About her shoulders was draped a black shawl, its fringes lost in the folds of her simple gown.

"Oh, Amalia!" cried the woman, "has this boy of yours given up his money yet?"

"No, mother, he has promised to wait till I come back. Marco is like a wild man when I talk. I thought Luigi would speak to him if I asked him. Please, dear Luigi, do not let him lose his money. We are ruined if he bets on Francesco."

Luigi reached out his hand and drew the girl toward him. His own daughter at home had just such a look in her eyes whenever she was in trouble and came to him for help.

"How much will he bet, child?" he asked in a low voice.

"Every soldo he has. Cavalli talks to him all the

131

time. They are like crazy people over there at the Beneto. Ah, good Luigi, do not win! I am so unhappy!" and the tears gathered in her eyes.

Luigi, still holding her hand, laughed gently as he looked up into her face. The others who had heard the girl's plea laughed with him.

"Go, child, and bring Marco here to me. Cavalli shall not ruin you both, if I can help it."

The girl pushed her hair back from her flushed face, drew her shawl closer about her shoulders, bent her pretty head, wormed her way out of the dense throng pressing in upon the table, and ran with all her might toward the Caffè Beneto, followed by her mother.

In a few minutes the two were back again, their arms fast locked in those of a young fellow of twenty—they marry young under Italian suns— who stood looking at Luigi with curious, wondering eyes. Not that he did not know the champion— every man in Venice knew him—but because Cavalli had pictured Luigi as of doubtful strength, and the Luigi before him did not fit Cavalli's measure.

"Marco," said Luigi, a smile crossing his face.

"Yes, Signore Zanaletto," answered the boy.

"Come nearer."

The young fellow advanced to the table. The others who had been near enough to learn of the girl's errand crowded the closer. Every utterance of a champion on a day like this is of value.

"You should be at work, boy, not betting on the race. You earn your living with your hands; that is better than Cavalli's way; he earns his with his tongue. I am nearly twice your age and have rowed many times, but I have never yet wagered as much as a soldo on any race of mine. Give your money to the good mother, and let her take it to the Pietà and get your boat. You will need it before the month is out, she tells me."

The boy hung his head and did not answer.

"Why do you think I shall lose? Have I not won four already?"

"Yes, but every year the signore gets older; you are not so strong as you were. And then, no man has won five races in fifty years. It is the Nicolletti's year to win, Cavalli says."

A cheer here went up from the outside of the

crowd. Some of the Nicolletti who had followed the boy had been listening.

"Cavalli should read his history better. It is not fifty years, but sixty. But we Italians work for ourselves now, and are free. That counts for something."

"Francesco works, Signore Zanaletto. He has arms like my leg."

"Yes, and for that reason you think him the stronger?"

"I did when Cavalli talked to me. Now I am in doubt."

The cheer that answered this reply came from some Castellani standing in the door of the caffè. When the cheering slackened a man on the outside of the crowd called out:

"Your Luigi is a coward. He will not bet because he knows he'll lose."

At this a big stevedore from the salt warehouse lunged toward Luigi and threw a silver lira on his table.

"Match that for Francesco!" he cried.

Luigi pushed it back.

"When I bet it will be with my equal," he said, icily.

A laugh of derision followed, in which Marco joined. The boy evidently thought the champion was afraid to risk his own money and make his word good. Boys of twenty often have such standards.

"Bet with Francesco, then, Signore Zanaletto," cried the stevedore. "He is twice your equal."

"Yes, bring him here," answered Luigi, quietly.

Half a dozen men, led by the big stevedore, made a rush for the Caffè Beneto. While they were gone, Marco, with Amalia and her mother, kept their places beside Luigi's table, chatting together in low tones. Luigi's refusal to bet with the stevedore and his willingness to bet with his opponent had unsettled Marco's mind all the more. Marriage, with him as with most of the people of his class, meant just money enough to pay the priest and to defray expenses of existence for a month. He would take his chances after that. They might both go to work again then, she back to her beads and he to his boat, but they would have had their holiday, and

135

a holiday is the one thing valued above all others by most Venetians. Should he lose, however, he must give up the girl for the present—the prettiest in all the quarter. And then perhaps Beppo Cavalli's son might find favor again in her eyes.

Amalia's anxiety was none the less keen. She had thrown over Cavalli's son for Marco, and if anything should go wrong the whole quarter would laugh at her. The two continued to ply Luigi with questions: as to who would win the toss for position; whether the wind would be against them; whether the water would be rough where the tide cut around the point of San Giorgio—all of which Marco, being a good boatman, could have settled for himself had his mind been normal. As they talked on, Luigi read their minds. Reason and common sense had evidently made no impression on the boy; he was not to be influenced in that way. Something stronger and more obvious, some demonstration that he could understand, was needed. Amalia's mother was his friend, and had been for years; what he could do to help her he would, no matter at what cost.

The throng parted again, and the stevedore, out of breath, forced his way into the circle.

"The great Francesco says he comes at no man's call. He is a Nicolletti. If any Castellani wants to see him he must come to *him*. He will wait for you at the Beneto."

A shout went up, and a rush to avenge the insult was only stopped by Luigi gaining his feet and raising his hand.

"Tell him," he said, in a clear voice, loud enough for everyone to hear, "that there is no need of his saying he is a Nicolletti; we would know it from his message. Come, boy, I'll show you of what stuff this gentleman is made."

The crowd fell back, Luigi striding along, his hand on Marco's shoulder. The champion could hardly conceal a smile of triumph as he neared the door of the Caffè Beneto, which opened to let them in. The two passed through the long passage into the room opening out on the veranda and the water beyond. Francesco sat at a table with his back to a window, sipping a glass of wine diluted with water. Cavalli, his head bound with a yellow hand-

137

kerchief, the colors of the Nicolletti, a scowl on his face, sat beside him. Every inch of standing room was blocked with his admirers.

"Signore Francesco," said Luigi, courteously, removing his hat, "I understand that you want to lose some money on the race. I have come to accommodate you. How much shall it be?"

"Ten lire!" cried one of the officers of the regatta, pouring some silver beside Francesco's hand as it rested on the table. "Put your money here, Signore Zanaletto. Our good landlord will hold the stakes."

"The money is not enough," answered Luigi. "I am the challenged party, and have the right to choose. Is it not so?"

"Yes, yes," cried half a dozen voices; "make it fifty lire! We are not *lazagnoni*. We have money —plenty of it. See, Signore Castellani"—and half a dozen palms covered with small coin were extended.

"I can choose, then, the kind of money and the sum," continued Luigi.

"Yes, gold, silver, paper—anything you want!"

138

"Then, gentle Nicolletti," said Luigi, in his softest and most courteous voice, "if you will permit me, I will choose the poor man's money. Match this, Signore Francesco," and he threw a copper soldo (a coin the size and thickness of an English penny) upon the table. "It is yours if you win."

A roar of laughter greeted the announcement. Francesco sprang to his feet.

"I am not here to be made a fool of! I don't bet with soldi! I throw them to beggars!" he cried, angrily.

"Pardon me, signore. Was it not agreed that I had the choice?"

Some muttering was heard at this, but no one answered.

"Let us see your soldo, then, signore," continued Luigi. "The race is the thing, not the money. A soldo is as good as a gold piece with which to back one's opinions. Come, I am waiting."

Francesco thrust his hand into his pocket, hauled up a handful of small coin, picked out a soldo and threw it contemptuously on the table.

"There—will that do?"

Luigi picked up the copper coin, examined it carefully, and tossed it back on the table.

"It is not of the right kind, signore. The stamp is wrong. We Castellani are very particular as to what money we wager and win."

The crowd craned their heads. If it was a counterfeit, they would put up another. This, however, did not seem to be Luigi's meaning. The boy Marco was so absorbed in the outcome that he reached forward to pick up the coin to examine it the closer when Luigi stopped him with his hand.

"What's the matter with the soldo?" growled Francesco, scrutinizing the pieces, "isn't it good?"

"Good enough, perhaps, for beggars, signore, and good enough, no doubt, for Nicolletti. But it lacks the stamp of the Castellani. Hand it to me, please, and I will put the mark of my guild upon it. Look, good Signore Francesco!"

As he spoke, Luigi caught the coin between his thumb and forefinger, clutched it with a grip of steel, and with a twist of his thumb bent the copper soldo to the shape of a watch crystal!

"That kind of a soldo, signore," he said in a low tone, as he tossed the concave coin back upon the table. "Match it, please! Here, try your fingers on my coin! Come, I am waiting. You do not answer, Signore Francesco. Why did you send for me, then? Had I known that your money was not ready I would not have left my caffè. Perhaps, however, some other distinguished Nicolletti can find some money good enough with which to bet a Castellani," and he looked about him. "No? I am sorry, gentlemen, very sorry. Addio!" and he picked up the bent coin, slipped it into his pocket, bowed like a doge to the room, and passed out through the door.

.   .   .   .

In the dense mass that lined the wall of the Public Gardens a girl and her lover stood with anxious eyes and flushed, hot cheeks, watching the home-stretch of the two contestants.

Francesco and Luigi, cheered by the shouts of a thousand throats, had reached the stake-boat off the Lido and were now swinging back to the goal of the Garden wall, both bending to their blades,

Luigi half a length behind, Francesco straining every nerve. Waves of red and of gold—the colors of the two guilds—surged and flashed from out the mass of spectators as each oarsman would gain or lose an inch.

Behind the lover and the girl stood the girl's mother, her black shawl twisted into a scarf. This she waved as heartily as the youngest about her.

"Don't cry, you fools!" she stopped long enough to shout in Amalia's ear. "It is his old way. Wait till he reaches the red buoy. Ah! what did I tell you! Luigi! Luigi! Bravo Castellani! See, Marco—see! Ah, Signore Francesco, your wind is gone, is it? You should nurse bambinos with those big arms of yours. Ah, look at him! Amalia, what did I tell you, you two fools!"

Marco did not answer. He was holding on to the marble coping of the wall, his teeth set, his lips quivering, his eyes fixed on Francesco's body in silhouette against the glistening sea. Luigi's long swing, rhythmical as a machine's, graceful as the curves of a wind sail, did not seem to interest him.

The boy had made his bet, and he would abide by it, but he would not tell the mother until the race was won. He had had enough of her tongue.

Suddenly Luigi clenched his thumb and forefinger tight about the handle of his oar, and with the sweep of a yacht gaining her goal headed straight for the stake-post, in full sight of the thousands lining the walls.

A great shout went up. Red flags, red parasols, rags, blankets, anything that told of Luigi's colors, rose and fluttered in the sunlight.

"*Primo! Primo!*" yelled the crowd. "Viva Castellani! Viva Zanaletto!"

Then, while the whole concourse of people held their breaths, their hearts in their mouths, Luigi with his fingers turned to steel, shot past Francesco with the dash of a gull, and amid the shouts of thousands lifted his victorious hat to the multitude.

For the first time in sixty years the same pair of arms had won five races!

Luigi was *Primo* and the Castellani the victors of the sea.

.   .   .   .

When Luigi's boat had reached the main landing of the Gardens and he had mounted the great flight of marble steps, a hundred hands held out to him joyous welcome. Amalia, who had forced her way to his side, threw her arms about his neck.

"Did the boy bet, child?" he asked, wiping the sweat from his face.

"Yes, signore."

"On Francesco?"

"No, dear Luigi, on you! Oh, I am so happy!"

"And what changed his mind?"

"The soldo!"

"The soldo! That makes me happy, too. Add it to your dowry, child," and he placed the coin in her hand.

She wears it now as a charm. The good priest blessed it with her wedding-ring.

A POINT OF HONOR

A POINT OF HONOR

I

THE omnibus stopped in the garden, or, to be
more exact, at the porch of the hotel opening into
the garden. Not the ordinary omnibus with a flap-
ping door fastened with a strap leading to the
boot-leg of the man on top, a post-office box inside with a glass front, holding a smoky kerosene
lamp, and two long pew-cushioned seats placed so
close together that everybody rubs everybody else's
knees when it is full; not that kind of an omnibus
at all, but a wide, low, yellow-painted (yellow as
a canary), morocco-cushioned, go-to-the-theatre-in
kind of an omnibus drawn by a pair of stout Nor-
mandy horses, with two men in livery on the box in
front and another on the lower step behind who
helps you in and out and takes your bundles and
does any number of delightful and courteous
things.

This yellow-painted chariot, moreover, was just the kind of a vehicle that should have moved in and out of this flower-decked garden. Not only did its color harmonize with the surroundings—quite as a mass of yellow nasturtiums harmonizes with the peculiar soft green of its leaves—but its appointments were quite in keeping with the luxury and distinction of the place. For only millionnaires and princes, and people who travel with valets and maids, and now and then a staid old painter like myself who is willing to be tucked away anywhere, but whose calling is supposed to lend éclat to the register, are ever to be found there.

The omnibus, then, stopped at the hotel porch and in front of the manager, who stood with a bunch of telegrams in his hand. Behind him smiled the clerk, and on his right bowed the Lord High Porter in gold lace and buttons: everything is done in the best and most approved style at the Baur au Lac in Zurich.

"Did you telegraph, sir? No? Well—let—me—see— Ah, yes! I remember—you were here last year. Number 13, Fritz, on the second floor" (this

to a boy), and the manager passed on and saluted
the other passengers—two duchesses in silk dusters,
a count in a straw hat with a green ribbon, and two
Italian nobleman in low collars and mustaches. At
least, they must have been noblemen or something
better, judging from the profundity of the manager's bow and the alacrity with which Fritz, the
boy, let go my bag and picked up three of theirs.

Another personage now stepped up—a little man
with the eyes of a fox—a courier whom I had not
seen for years.

) "Why, Joseph! where did you drop from?" I
asked.

"From the Engadine, my Lord, and I hope your
Lordship is most well."

"Pretty well, Joseph. What are you doing
here?"

"It is an Englishman—a lame Englishman—a
matter of two weeks only. And you, my Lord?"

"Just from Venice, on my way back to Paris," I
answered.

By this time the manager was gazing with his
eyes twice their size, and the small boy was stand-

ing in the middle of a heap of bags, wondering which one of the nobilities (including myself) he would serve first.

Joseph had now divested me of my umbrella and sketch-trap and was facing the manager.

"Did I hear that thirteen was the number of his Lordship's room?" he inquired of that gentleman. "I will myself go. Give me the bag" (this to the boy). "This way, my Lord." And he led the way through the cool hall filled with flowering plants and up a staircase panelled with mirrors. I followed contentedly behind.

Joseph and I are old acquaintances. In my journeyings around Europe I frequently run across him. He and I have had some varied experiences together in our time—the first in Milan at the Hotel Imperial. A young bride and groom, friends of mine—a blue-eyed, sweet-faced young girl with a husband but one year her senior (the two with a £2,000 letter of credit, the gift of a doting father) —had wired for rooms for the night at the Imperial. It was about eight o'clock when the couple drove up in one of those Italian hacks cut low-neck

A POINT OF HONOR

—a landau really—with coachman and footman on the box, and Joseph in green gloves and a silk hat on the front seat. My personal salutations over, we all mounted the stairs, preceded by the entire staff with the proprietor at their head. Here on the first landing we were met by two flunkeys in red and a blaze of electric light which revealed five rooms. In one was spread a game supper with every variety of salad known to an Italian lunch-counter; in another—the salon—stood a mass of roses the size and shape of an oleander in full bloom; then came a huge bedroom, a bathroom and a boudoir.

The groom, young as he was, knew how little was left of the letter of credit. The bride did not. Neither did Joseph.

"What's all this for, Hornblend?" asked the groom, casting his eyes about in astonishment. Hornblend is the other half of Joseph's name.

"For Monsieur and Madame."

"What, for *one night?*"

Joseph worked both shoulders and extended his red fingers—he had removed his gloves—till they looked like two bunches of carrots.

"Does it not Monsieur please?"

"Please! Do you think I'm a royal family?"

The carrots collapsed, the shoulders stopped, and a pained expression overspread Joseph's countenance. The criticisms had touched his heart.

The groom and I put our heads together—mine is gray, and I have seen many couriers in my time. His was blond and curly, and Joseph was his first experience.

I beckoned to the proprietor.

"Who ordered this suite of rooms and all this tomfoolery?"

The man bowed and waved his hand loftily toward the groom.

"How?"

"By telegraph."

"Let me see the despatch."

One of the functionaries—the clerk—handed me the document.

"Is this the only one?"

"Yes."

"It is signed 'Joseph Hornblend,' you see."

"Yes."

A POINT OF HONOR

"Then let Hornblend pay for it. Now be good enough to show these young people to a bedroom, and send your head-waiter to me. We will all dine downstairs together in the café."

Since that night in Milan Joseph always has called me "my Lord."

He had altered but little. His legs were perhaps more bowed, the checks of his trousers a trifle larger, and the part in his iron-gray hair less regular than in the old days, but the general effect was the same —the same flashy waistcoat, the same long gold watch-chain baited with charms, the same shiny, bell-crown silk hat, and the same shade of green kid gloves—same pair, I think. Nor had his manner changed—that cringing, deferential, attentive manner which is so flattering at first to the unsuspecting and inexperienced, and so positive and top-lofty when his final accounts are submitted—particularly if they are disputed. The voice, too, had lost none of its soft, purring quality—a church-whisper-voice with the drone of the organ in it.

And yet withal Joseph is not a bad fellow. Once

153

he knows the size of your pocket-book he willingly adapts his expenditures to its contents. Ofttimes, it is true, there is nothing left but the pocket-book, but then some couriers would take that. When he is in doubt as to the amount, he tries experiments. I have learned since that the lay-out for the bride and groom that night in Milan was only one of his experiments—the proprietor being co-conspirator. The coach belonged to the hotel; the game supper was moved up from the restaurant, and the flowers had been left over from a dinner the night before. Had they all done duty, Joseph's commissions would have been that much larger. As it was, he collected his percentage only on the coach and the two men on the box and the flunkeys at the head of the stairs. These had been *used*. The other preparations were only looked at.

Then again, Joseph not only speaks seven languages, but he speaks them well—for Joseph— so much so that a stranger is never sure of his nationality.

"Are you French, Joseph?" I once asked him. "No."

A POINT OF HONOR

"Dutch?"

"No."

"What, then?"

"I am a Jew gentleman from Germany."

He lied, of course. He's a Levantine from Constantinople, with Greek, Armenian, Hindu, and perhaps some Turkish blood in his veins. This combination insures him good temper, capacity, and imagination—not a bad mixture for a courier. Besides, he is reasonably honest—not punctiliously so —not as to francs, perhaps, but certainly as to fifty-pound notes—that is, he was while he served me. Of course, I never had a fifty-pound note— not all at once—but if I had had I don't think he would have absorbed it—not if I had signed it on the back for identification and had kept it in a money-belt around my waist and close to my skin.

Those things, however, never trouble me. I don't want to make a savings-bank of Joseph. It is his vivid imagination that appeals to me, or perhaps the picturesqueness with which he puts things. In this he is a veritable master. His material, too, is

not only uncommonly rich, but practically inex-
haustible. He knows everybody; has travelled with
everybody; has always kept one ear and one eye
open even when asleep, and has thus picked up an
immense amount of information regarding people
and events—mostly his own patrons—the telling of
which has served to enliven many a quiet hour while
he sat beside me as I painted. Why, once I remember in Stamboul, when some Arabs had——

But I forget that I am following Joseph upstairs, and that his mission is to see that I am comfortably lodged at the Baur au Lac in Zurich.

When we reached the second floor Joseph met the
porter emerging into the corridor with my large
luggage. He had mounted the back stairs.

"Let me see Number 13, porter," cried Joseph.
"Ah, yes—it is just as I supposed. Is it in that hole
you would put my Lord—where there is noise all
the time? You see that window, my Lord?" (By
this time I had reached the two disputants and had
entered the room.) "You remember, your Highness,
that enormous omnibus in which you have arrived
just? It is there that it sleeps." And Joseph craned

156

his head out of the window and pointed in the direction of the court-yard. "When it goes out in the morning at seven o'clock for the train it is like thunder. The Count Monflot had this room. You should have seen him when he was awoke at seven. He was like a crazy man. He pulled all the strings out of the bells, and when the waiter come he had the hat-box of Monsieur the Count at his head."

Dismissing the apartment with a contemptuous wave of his hand, Joseph, with the porter's assistance, who had a pass-key, began a search of the other vacant rooms: half the hotel was vacant, I afterward learned; all this telegram and book business was merely an attempt to bolster up the declining days of a bad season.

"Number 21? No—it is a little better, but it's too near the behind stairs. It would be absurd to put his Lordship there. Number 24?"—here he looked into another room. "No, you can hear the grande baggage in the night going up and down. No, it will not do."

The manager, having disposed of the other members of the Emperor's household, now approached with a servile smile fitted to all parts of his face. Joseph attacked him at once.

"Is his Lordship a valet, Monsieur, that you should put him in such holes? Do you not know that he never wakes until ten, and has his coffee at eleven, and the omnibus, you know, sleeps there?" And he pointed outside. (Another Levantine lie: I am up at seven when the light is right.)

Here the porter unlocked another room and stood by smiling. He knew the game was up now, and had reserved this one for the last.

"Number—28! Ah, this is something like. Yes, my Lord, this will be quite right. La Contessa Moriarti had this room—yes, I remember." (Joseph never serves any woman below the rank of contessa.)

So I moved into Number 28, handed Joseph the keys, and the porter deposited my luggage and withdrew, followed by the manager. Soon the large and small trunks were disembowelled, my sponge hung on a nail in the window, and the several toilet articles distributed in their proper places, Joseph serving in the triple capacity of courier, valet, and chambermaid—the lame Englishman being out driving, and Joseph, therefore, having this hour to himself. This distribution, of course, was made in deference to my exalted rank and the ten-franc gold piece which he never fails to get despite my resolutions, and which he always seems to have earned despite my knowledge as to how the trick is performed.

Suddenly a crash sounded through the hall as if somebody had dropped a tray of dishes. Then came another, and another. Either every waiter in the house was dropping trays, or an attack was being made on the pantry by a mob.

Joseph, with a bound, threw back the door and we rushed out.

Just opposite my room was a small salon with the door wide open. In its centre stood a man with an iron poker in his hand. He was busy smashing what was left of a large mirror, its pieces littering the floor. On the sofa lay another man twice the size of the first one, who was roaring with laughter. Down the corridor swooped a collection of guests, porters,

159

and chambermaids in full cry, the manager at their head.

"Two hundred and fifty francs, eh—for a looking-glass worth twenty francs?" I heard the man with the poker shout. "I blister with my gas-jet one little corner, and I must pay two hundred and fifty francs. I have ruined the mirror, have I, eh? And it must be thrown out and a new one put in to-morrow—eh?" Bang! bang! Here the poker came down on some small fragment still clinging to the frame. "Yes, it *will* come out [bang!]—*all* of it will come out."

The manager was now trying to make himself heard. Such words as "my mirror," "outrage," "Gendarme," could be heard above the sound of the breaking glass and the shrieks of the man on the sofa, who seemed to be in a paroxysm of laughter.

I looked on for a moment. Some infuriated lodger, angry, perhaps, at the overcharge in his bill, was venting his wrath on the furniture. It was not my mirror, and it was not my bill; the manager was present with staff enough to throw both men downstairs if he pleased and without my assistance, and so I turned and reentered my room. Two things fixed themselves in my mind: the alert figure, trim as a fencer's, of the man with the poker, and the laugh of the fat man sprawling on the lounge.

Joseph followed me into my room and shut the door softly behind him.

"Ah, I knew it was he. No other man is so crazy like that. He would break the head of the propriétaire just the same. That is an old swindle. That mirror has been cracked four—five—six times. The gas-jet is fixed so that you *must* crack it. All the mirrors like the one he burnt—it was only a little spot—go upstairs in the cheap rooms and new ones are brought in for such games. 'Most always they pay, but monsieur—it is not like him to pay. He has heard of the trick, perhaps—is it not delicious?" and Joseph's face widened into a grin.

"You know him, then?" I broke in.

"Know him?—oh, for many years. He is the great Doctor Barsac. He smashes everything he

doesn't like. He smashed that old fat monsieur who
made so much laugh. His name is Mariguy. He
looks like a curé, does he not? But he is not a curé;
he is an advocate. Barsac is from Basle, but Mariguy lives in Paris. Those two are never separated;
they love each other like a man and a wife. There
is a great medical convention here in Zurich, and
Barsac has brought Mariguy with him to show him
off. He put a new silver stomach in Mariguy last
winter and is very proud of it. It is the great operation of the year, they say."

"What happened to the fat man, Joseph—was
it an accident?"

"No—a duel. Barsac ran him through the belly
with his sword."

"Permit me, my Lord—" And Joseph stepped
to the window. "Yes, there comes the lame Englishman home from the drive. Excuse me—I will go
and help him from his carriage." And Joseph bowed
himself out backward.

．　　．　　．　　．　　．　　．　　．

A POINT OF HONOR

II

Joseph's departure left my mind in an unsettled state. I hadn't the slightest interest in the
great surgeon who had made the cure of the year,
nor in the stout advocate with his nickel-plated di-
gestive apparatus. Both of them might have broken
every mirror in the hotel and have thrown the fragments out of the window, and the manager after
them, without raising my pulse a beat. Neither did
the medical convention nor the doctor's exhibit
cause me a moment's thought. Such things were
commonplace and of every-day occurrence. Only
the dramatic in life appeals to so staid and gray an
old painter as myself, and even Joseph's pictur-
esque imagination could not imbue either one of
the incidents of the morning with that desirable
quality.

What really did appeal to me as I conjured up
in my mind the picture of the fat man sprawled
over the sofa-cushions roaring with laughter was

the duel and the causes that led up to it. Why, if the man was his friend, had the doctor selected the hilarious advocate as an antagonist, and what could have induced the surgeon to pick out that particular section of his friend's surface in which to insert his sword.

That same night, in the smoking-room of the hotel, Joseph caught sight of me as he passed the open door and moved forward to my table. He had changed his dress of the morning, discarding the inflammatory waistcoat, and was now upholstered in a full suit of black. He explained that there were some friends of his living in the village who were going to have some music. The Englishman was in bed and asleep, and now that he was sure that I was comfortable, he could give himself some little freedom, with his mind at rest.

I motioned him to a seat.

He laid his silk hat and one glove on an adjoining table, spread his coat-tails, and deposited himself on the extreme edge of a chair—a position which would enable him to regain his feet at a moment's notice should any of my friends chance to

164

join me. It is just such delicate recognition of my rank and lordly belongings that makes Joseph's companionship ofttimes a pleasure.

"You tell me, Joseph, that that crazy doctor stabbed the fat man in a duel."

, "Not *stabbed*, my Lord! That is not the nice word. It was done so—*so*—so." And Joseph's wrist, holding an imaginary sword, performed the grand thrust in the air. "He is a master with the rapier. When he was at the Sorbonne he had five duels and never once a scratch. His honor was most paramount. He would fight with anybody, and for the smallest thing—if one man had a longer cane, or wore a higher hat, or took cognac in his coffee. Not for the grisette or for the cards in the face; not so big a thing as that; quite a small thing that nobody would remember a moment. And with his friends always—never with the man he did not before know."

"And was the fat man his friend?"

"His friend! Mon Dieu! they were like the brothers. One—two—five year, I think—all the whole time of the instruction. I was not there, of

165

course, but a friend of mine tell me—a most truthful man, my friend."

"What was the row about? Cognac in his coffee?"

"I do not know—perhaps somethings. Yes, I do remember now. It was the cutting of the hair. Barsac like it short and Mariguy like it long. Barsac tried to cut the hair from Mariguy's head when he was asleep, and then it began. It was in that little wood at the bridge at Surèsne that they went to fight. You know you turn to the right and there is a little place—all small trees—there it was.

"When they all got ready, there quickly arrive a carriage all dust, and the horse in a sweat, and out jumps an old lady—it was Mariguy's mother. Somebody had told her—not Mariguy, of course, but some student. 'Stop!' she cried; 'you do not my son kill. You, Barsac, you do nothing but fight!' Then they all talk, and Mariguy say to Barsac, 'It cannot be; my mother, as you see, is old. There is no one but me. If I am wounded, she will be in the bed with fright. If I am killed, she will be dead. It is my mother, you see, that you fight, not me.'

A POINT OF HONOR

"Barsac take off his hat and bow to madame."
(Joseph had now reached for his own and was
illustrating the incident with an appropriate gesture.) " 'Madame Mariguy,' said Barsac, 'I make
ten thousand pardons. I respect the devotion of the
mother,' and he went back to Paris, and Mariguy
got into the carriage and go away with the
mother."

"But, Joseph, of course that was not the last
of it?"

"Yes, my Lord, until one year ago."

"Why, did they have another quarrel, Joseph?"

"No, not another—never but that one. They
were for a long time what you call friends of the
bosom. Every day after that they see each other,
and every night they dine at the Louis d'Or below
the Luxembourg. Then pretty soon the doctor, he
have to take his degree and come back to Basle to
live, and Monsieur Mariguy also have take his
degree and become a great advocate in Paris.
Every week come a letter from Barsac to Mariguy,
and one from Mariguy to Barsac."

Joseph stopped in his narrative at this point,

noticing perhaps some shade of incredulity across my countenance, and said parenthetically: "I am quite surprised, my Lord, that you have not this heard before. It was quite the talk of Paris at the time. No? Well, then, I will tell you everything as it did happen, for I do assure you that it is most exciting.

"All this time—it was quite ten years, perhaps fifteen—not one word does Monsieur Barsac say to Monsieur Mariguy about the insult of the long hair. All the time, too, they are together. For the summer they go to a little village in the Swiss mountains, and for the winter they go to Nice, and 'most every night they play a little at the tables. It was there I met them.

"One morning at Basle the doctor was at his table eating the breakfast when the newspaper is put on the side. He read a little and sip his coffee, and then he read a little more—all this, my Lord, was in the papers at the time—I am quite astonished that you have not seen it—and then the doctor make a loud cry, and throw the paper down, run

168

upstairs, pack his bag, jump into a fiacre and go like mad to the station. The next morning he is in Paris, and at the house of his friend Mariguy. In three days they are at Surèsne again—not in the little wood, but in the garden of Monsieur Rochefort, who was his second. It was against the law to go into the little wood to fight, so they took the nearest place to their old meeting—a small sentiment, you see, my Lord, which Monsieur the Doctor always enjoys.

"They toss up for the sun, and Monsieur Barsac he gets the shade. At the first pass, no one is hurt. At the second, Monsieur Barsac has a little scratch on his wrist, but no blood. The seconds make inspection most careful. They regret that the encounter must go on, but the honor is not yet satisfied. At the third, Monsieur Mariguy made a misstep, and Monsieur Barsac's sword go into Monsieur Mariguy's shirt and come out at Monsieur Mariguy's back.

"You can imagine what then take place. Doctor Barsac cry in a loud voice that his honor is satisfied, and the next moment he is on his knees beside his friend. Monsieur Mariguy is at once put in the bed, and for one—two—three months he is dead one day and breathe a little the next. Barsac never leave the house of his friend Monsieur Rochefort one moment —not one day does he go back to Basle. Every night he is by the bed of Monsieur Mariguy. Then comes the critical moment. Monsieur Mariguy must have a new stomach; the old one is like a stocking with a hole in the toe. Then comes the great triumph of Monsieur le Docteur. All Paris come out to see. To make a stomach of silver is to make one the fool, they say. The old doctors shake their heads, but Barsac he only laugh. In one more month Monsieur Mariguy is on his feet, and every day walks a little in the Bois near the house of Monsieur Rochefort. In one more month he run, and eat himself full like a boy.

"He is now no longer the great advocate. He is the *example* of Monsieur Barsac. That is why he is here at the medical convention. They arrived only yesterday and leave to-night. If you turn a little, my Lord, you can see into the other room. There they sit smoking.—Ah! do you hear? That is Monsieur Mariguy's laugh. Oh, they enjoy themselves! They have drank two bottles of Johannisberger already—twenty-five francs each, if you please, my Lord. The head waiter showed me the bottles. But what does Barsac care? He cut everything out of the insides of the Prince Morin one day last month, and had for a fee fifty thousand francs and the order of St. John."

I bent my head in the direction of Joseph's index finger and easily recognized the two men at the table. The smaller man, Barsac, was even more trim and alert-looking than when I caught a glimpse of him in the bedroom. As he sat and talked to Mariguy he looked more like an officer in the French army than a doctor. His hair was short, his mustache pointed, and his beard closely trimmed. He had two square shoulders and a slim waist, and talked with his hands as if they were part of his mental equipment. The other man, Mariguy, the "example," was just a fat, jolly, good-natured Frenchman, who to all appearance loved a bottle of wine better than he did a brief.

Joseph was about to begin again when I stopped him with this inquiry:

"There is one thing in your story, Joseph, that I don't quite get: you say they were students together?"

"Yes, my Lord."

"That the first duel—the one that the mother stopped—was fifteen years ago?"

"Quite true, my Lord."

"And that this last duel was fought a year ago, and that all that time they were together whenever they could be, and devoted friends?"

"Every word true, my Lord."

"Well, then, why didn't they fight before?"

Joseph looked at me with a curious expression on his face—one rather of disappointment, as if I had utterly failed to grasp his meaning.

"Fight before! It would have been impossible, my Lord. Barsac's honor was at the stake."

"And he must wait fifteen years," I asked with some impatience, "to vindicate it?"

"Certainly, my Lord—or twice that time if it was necessary. It was only when he read in the

paper at the table of his breakfast that morning in
Basle that he knew."

"What difference did that make?"

"Every difference, my Lord; Madame Mariguy,
the mother, was only the day before dead."

SIMPLE FOLK

SIMPLE FOLK

A long reach of coast country, white and smooth, broken by undulating fences smothered in snow-drifts, only their stakes and bush-tops showing; farther away, horizontal markings of black pines; still farther away, a line of ragged dunes bearded with yellow grass bordering a beach flecked with scurries of foam—mouthings of a surf twisting as if in pain; beyond this a wide sea, greenish gray, gray and gray-blue, slashed here and there with white-caps pricked by wind rapiers; beyond this again, out into space, a leaden sky flat as paint and as monotonous.

Nearer by, so close that I could see their movements from the car window, spatterings of crows, and higher up circling specks of gulls glinting or darkening as their breasts or backs caught the light. These crows and gulls were the only things alive in the wintry waste.

No, one thing more—two, in fact: as I came nearer the depot, a horse tethered to the section of the undulating fence, a rough-coated, wind-blown, shackly beast; the kind the great Schreyer always painted shivering with cold outside a stable door (and in the snow, too), and a man: Please remember, A MAN! And please continue to remember it to the end of this story.

Thirty-one years in the service he—this keeper of the Naukashon Life-Saving Station—twenty-five at this same post. Six feet and an inch, tough as a sapling and as straight; long-armed, long-legged, broad-shouldered and big-boned; face brown and tanned as skirt leather; eye like a hawk's; mouth but a healed scar, so firm is it; low-voiced, simple-minded and genuine.

If you ask him what he has done in all these thirty-one years of service he will tell you:

"Oh, I kind o' forget; the Superintendent gets reports. You see, some months we're not busy, and then ag'in we ain't had no wrecks for considerable time."

If you should happen to look in his locker, away back out of sight, you would perhaps find a small paper box, and in it a gold medal—the highest his government can give him—inscribed with his name and a record of some particular act of heroism. When he is confronted with the tell-tale evidence, he will say:

"Oh, yes—they *did* give me that! I'm keepin' it for my grandson."

If you, failing to corkscrew any of the details out of him, should examine the Department's reports, you will find out all he "forgets"—among them the fact that in his thirty-one years of service he and the crew under him have saved the lives of one hundred and thirty-one men and women out of a possible one hundred and thirty-two. He explains the loss of this unlucky man by saying apologetically that "the fellow got dizzy somehow and locked himself in the cabin, and we didn't know he was there until she broke up and he got washed ashore."

This was the man who, when I arrived at the railroad station, held out a hand in hearty welcome, his own closing over mine with the grip of a cant-hook.

"Well, by Jiminy! Superintendent said you was

comin', but I kind o' thought you wouldn't 'til the weather cleared. Gimme yer bag—Yes, the boys are all well and will be glad to see ye. Colder than blue blazes, ain't it? Snow ain't over yet. Well, well, kind o' natural to see ye!"

The bag was passed up; the Captain caught the reins in his crab-like fingers, and the bunch of wind-blown fur, gathering its stiffened legs together, wheeled sharply to the left and started in to make pencil-markings in double lines over the white snow seaward toward the Naukashon Life-Saving Station.

The perspective shortened: first the smooth, unbroken stretch; then the belt of pines; then a flat marsh diked by dunes; then a cluster of black dots, big and little—the big one being the Station house, and the smaller ones its outbuildings and fishermen's shanties; and then the hard, straight line of the pitiless sea.

I knew the "boys." I had known some of them for years: ever since I picked up one of their stations—its site endangered by the scour of the tide —ran it on skids a mile over the sand to the land

Over the white snow seaward.

side of the inlet without moving the crew or their comforts (even their wet socks were left drying on a string by the kitchen stove); shoved it aboard two scows timbered together, started out to sea under the guidance of a light-draught tug in search of its new location three miles away, and then, with the assistance of a suddenly developed north-east gale, backed up by my own colossal engineering skill, dropped the whole concern—skids, house, kitchen stove, socks and all—into the sea. When the surf dogs were through with its carcass the beach was strewn with its bones picked clean by their teeth. Only the weathercock, which had decorated its cupola, was left. This had floated off and was found perched on top of a sand-dune, whizzing away on its ornamental cap as merry as a jig-dancer. It was still whirling away, this time on the top of the cupola at Naukashon. I could see it plainly as I drove up, its arrow due east, looking for trouble as usual.

Hence my friendship for Captain Shortrode and his trusty surfmen. Hence, too, my welcome when I pushed in the door of the sitting-room and caught the smell of the cooking: Dave Austin's clam chowder—I could pick it out anywhere, even among the perfumes of a Stamboul kitchen; and hence, too, the hearty hand-grasp from the big, brawny men around the stove.

"Well! Kind o' summer weather you picked out! Here, take this chair—Gimme yer coat.—Git them legs o' yourn in, Johnny. He's a new man—John Partridge; guess you ain't met him afore. Where's Captain Shortrode gone? Oh, yes!—puttin' up old Moth-eaten. Ain't nothin' he thinks as much of as that old horse. Oughter pack her in camphor. Well, how's things in New York?—Nelse, put on another shovel of coal—Yes, colder'n Christmas! . . . Nothin' but nor'east wind since the moon changed. . . . Chowder!—Yes, yer dead right; Dave's cookin' this week, and he said this mornin' he'd have a mess for ye."

A stamping of feet outside and two bifurcated walruses (four hours out on patrol) pushed in the door. Muffled in oilskins these, rubber-booted to their hips, the snow-line marking their waists where they had plunged through the drifts; their sou'-westers tied under their chins, shading beards white with frost and faces raw with the slash of the beach wind.

More hand-shakes now; and a stripping of wet outer-alls; a wash-up and a hair-smooth; a shout of "Dinner!" from the capacious lungs of David the cook; a silent, reverential grace with every head bowed (these are the things that surprise you until you know these men), and with one accord an attack is made upon Dave's chowder and his corn-bread and his fried ham and his— Well, the air was keen and bracing, and the salt of the sea a permeating tonic, and the smell!—Ah, David! I wish you'd give up your job and live with me, and bring your saucepan and your griddle and your broiler and—my appetite!

The next night the Captain was seated at the table working over his monthly report, the kerosene lamp lighting up his bronzed face and falling upon his open book. There is nothing a keeper hates to do so much as making out monthly reports; his hard, horny hand is shaped to grasp an oar, not a pen. Four other men were asleep upstairs in their bunks, waiting their turns to be called for patrol. Two were breasting a north-east gale howling along the coast, their Coston signals tightly buttoned under their oilskins.

Tom Van Brunt and I—Tom knew all about the little kitchen stove and the socks—he had forgiven me my share in their loss—were tilted back against the wall in our chairs. The slop and rattle of Dave's dishes came in through the open door leading to the kitchen. Outside could be heard the roar and hammer of the surf and the shriek of the baffled wind trying to burglarize the house by way of the eaves and the shutters.

The talk had drifted to the daily life at the Station; the dreariness of waiting for something to come ashore (in a disappointed tone from Tom, as if he and his fellow surfmen had not had their share of wrecks this winter); of the luck of Number 16, in charge of Captain Elleck and his crew, who had got seven men and a woman out of an English bark last week without wetting the soles of their feet.

184

SIMPLE FOLK

"Fust shot went for'd of her chain plates," Tom explained, "and then they made fast and come off in the breeches-buoy. Warn't an hour after she struck 'fore they had the hull of 'em up to the Station and supper ready. Heavy sea runnin' too."

Tom then shifted his pipe and careened his head my way, and with a tone in his voice that left a ring behind it which vibrated in me for days, and does now, said:

"I've been here for a good many years, and I guess I'll stay here long as the Guv'ment'll let me. Some people think we've got a soft snap, and some people think we ain't. 'Tis kind o' lonely, sometimes—then somethin' comes along and we even up; but it ain't that that hurts me really—it's bein' so much away from home."

Tom paused, rapped the bowl of his pipe on his heel to clear it, twisted his body so that he could lay the precious comfort on the window-sill behind him safe out of harm's way, and continued:

"Yes, bein' so much away from home. I've been a surfman, you know, goin' on thirteen years, and out o' that time I ain't been home but two year and

185

a half runnin' the days solid, which they ain't. I live up in Naukashon village, and you know how close that is. Cap'n could 'a' showed you my house as you druv 'long through—it's just across the way from his'n.''

I looked at Tom in surprise. I knew that the men did not go home but once in two weeks, and then only for a day, but I had not summed up the vacation as a whole. Tom shifted his tilted leg, settled himself firmer in his chair, and went on:

"I ain't askin' no favors, and I don't expect to git none. We got to watch things down here, and we dasn't be away when the weather's rough, and there ain't no other kind 'long this coast; but now and then somethin' hits ye and hurts ye, and ye don't forgit it. I got a little baby at home—seven weeks old now—hearty little feller—goin' to call him after the Cap'n," and he nodded toward the man scratching away with his pen. "I ain't had a look at that baby but three times since he was born, and last Sunday it come my turn and I went up to see the wife and him. My brother Bill lives with me. He lost his wife two year ago, and the baby

she left didn't live more'n a week after she died,
and so Bill, not havin' no children of his own,
takes to mine—I got three."

Again Tom stopped, this time for a percept-
ible moment. I noticed a little quiver in his voice
now.

"Well, when I got home it was 'bout one o'clock
in the day. I been on patrol that mornin'—it was
snowin' and thick. Wife had the baby up to the
winder waitin' for me, and they all come out—
Bill and my wife and my little Susie, she's five
year old—and then we all went in and sat down,
and I took the baby in my arms, and it looked at
me kind o' skeered-like and cried; and Bill held
out his hands and took the baby, and he stopped
cryin' and laid kind o' contented in his arms, and
my little Susie said, 'Pop, I guess baby thinks
Uncle Bill's his father.' . . . *I—tell—you—
that—hurt!*"

As the last words dropped from Tom's lips two
of the surfmen—Jerry Potter and Robert Saul,
who had been breasting the north-east gale—pushed
open the door of the sitting-room and peered in,

looking like two of Nansen's men just off an ice-floe. Their legs were clear of snow this time, the two having brushed each other off with a broom on the porch outside. Jerry had been exchanging brass checks with the patrol of No. 14, three miles down the beach, and Saul had been setting his clock by a key, locked in an iron box bolted to a post two miles and a half away and within sight of the inlet. Tramping the beach beside a roaring surf in a north-east gale blowing fifty miles an hour, and in the teeth of a snow-storm each flake cutting like grit from a whirling grindstone, was to these men what the round of a city park is to a summer policeman.

Jerry peeled off his waterproofs from head, body, and legs; raked a pair of felt slippers from under a chair; stuck his stocking-feet into their comforting depths; tore a sliver of paper from the end of a worn-out journal, twisted it into a wisp, worked the door of the cast-iron stove loose with his marlin-spike of a finger, held the wisp to the blaze, lighted his pipe carefully and methodically; tilted a chair back, and settling his great frame comfortably between its arms, started in to smoke. Saul duplicated his movements to the minutest detail, with the single omission of those connected with the pipe. Saul did not smoke.

Up to this time not a word had been spoken by anybody since the two men entered. Men who live together so closely dispense with "How d'yes" and "Good-bys." I was not enough of a stranger to have the rule modified on my account after the first salutations.

Captain Shortrode looked up from his report and broke the silence.

"That sluice-way cuttin' in any, Jerry?"

Jerry nodded his head and replied between puffs of smoke:

" 'Bout fifty feet, I guess."

The grizzled Captain took off his eye-glasses— he only used them in making up his report—laid them carefully beside his sheet of paper, stretched his long legs, lifting his body to the perpendicular, dragged a chair to my side of the room, and said with a dry chuckle:

"I've got to laugh every time I think of that

189

sluice-way. Last month— Warn't it last month, Jerry?" Jerry nodded, and sent a curl of smoke through his ragged mustache, accompanied by the remark, "Yes—last month."

The Captain continued:

"Last month, I say, we were havin' some almighty high tides, and when they git to cuttin' round that sluice-way it makes it bad for our beach-cart, 'specially when we've got to keep abreast of a wreck that ain't grounded so we can git a line to her; so I went down after supper to see how the sluice-way was comin' on. It was foggy, and a heavy sea runnin'—the surf showin' white, but everythin' else black as pitch. Fust thing I knew I heared somethin' like the rattle of an oar-lock, or a tally-block, and then a cheer come just outside the breakers. I run down to the swash and listened, and then I seen her comin' bow on, big as a house; four men in her holdin' on to the gunnels, hollerin' for all they was worth. I got to her just as the surf struck her and rolled her over bottom-side up."

"Were you alone?" I interrupted.

"Had to be. The men were up and down the beach and the others was asleep in their bunks. Well, when I had 'em all together I run 'em up on the beach and in here to the Station, and when the light showed 'em up— Well, I tell ye, one of 'em—a nigger cook—was a sight! 'Bout seven feet high, and thick round as a flag-pole, and blacker'n that stove, and skeered so his teeth was a-chatterin'. They'd left their oyster schooner a-poundin' out on the bar and had tried to come ashore in their boat. Well, we got to work on 'em and got some dry clo'es on 'em, and——"

"Were you wet, too?" I again interrupted.

"Wet! Soppin'! I'd been under the boat feelin' 'round for 'em. Well, the King's Daughters had sent some clo'es down, and we looked over what we had, and I got a pair of high-up pants, and Jerry, who wears Number 12—Don't you, Jerry?" (Jerry nodded and puffed on)—"had an old pair of shoes, and we found a jacket, another high-up thing big 'nough to fit a boy, that come up to his shoulder-blades, and he put 'em on and then he set 'round here for a spell dryin' out, with his long black legs

191

stickin' from out of his pants like handle-bars, and his hands, big as hams, pokin' out o' the sleeves o' his jacket. We got laughin' so we had to go out by ourselves in the kitchen and have it out; didn't want to hurt his feelin's, you know."

The Captain leaned back in his chair, laughed quietly to himself at the picture brought back to his mind, and continued, the men listening quietly, the smoke of their pipes drifting over the room.

"Next mornin' we got the four of 'em all ready to start off to the depot on their way back to Philadelphy—there warn't no use o' their stayin', their schooner was all up and down the beach, and there was oysters 'nough 'long the shore to last everybody a month. Well, when the feller got his rig on he looked himself all over, and then he said he would like to have a hat. 'Bout a week before Tom here [Tom nodded now, and smiled] had picked up on the beach one o' these high gray stovepipe hats with a black band on it, blowed overboard from some o' them yachts, maybe. Tom had it up on the mantel there dryin', and he said he didn't care, and I give it to the nigger and off he started, and we all went out on the back porch to see him move. Well, sir, when he went up 'long the dunes out here toward the village, steppin' like a crane in them high-up pants and jacket and them Number 12s of Jerry's and that hat of Tom's 'bout three sizes too small for him, I tell ye he was a *show!*"

Jerry and Saul chuckled, and Tom broke into a laugh—the first smile I had seen on Tom's face since he had finished telling me about the little baby at home.

I laughed too—outwardly to the men and inwardly to myself with a peculiar tightening of the throat, followed by a glow that radiated heat as it widened. My mind was not on the grotesque negro cook in the assorted clothes. All I saw was a man fighting the surf, groping around in the blackness of the night for four water-soaked, terrified men until he got them, as he said, "all together." That part of it had never appealed to the Captain, and never will. Pulling drowning men, single-handed, from a boiling surf, was about as easy as pulling gudgeons out of a babbling brook.

Saul now piped up:

"Oughter git the Cap'n to tell ye how he got that lady ashore last winter from off that Jamaica brig."

At the sound of Saul's voice Captain Shortrode rose quickly from his chair, picked up his report and spectacles, and with a deprecating wave of his hand, as if the story would have to come from some other lips than his own, left the room—to "get an envelope," he said.

"He won't come back for a spell," laughed Jerry. "The old man don't like that yarn." "Old man" was a title of authority, and had nothing to do with the Captain's fifty years.

I made no comment—not yet. My ears were open, of course, but I was not holding the tiller of conversation and preferred that someone else should steer.

Again Saul piped up, this time to me, reading my curiosity in my eyes:

"Well, there warn't nothin' much to it, 'cept the way the Cap'n got her ashore," and again Saul chuckled quietly, this time as if to himself. "The

194

beach was full o' shipyard rats and loafers, and when they heared there was a lady comin' ashore in the breeches-buoy, more of 'em kept comin' in on the run. We'd fired the shot-line and had the anchor buried and the hawser fast to the brig's mast and the buoy rigged, and we were just goin' to haul in when Cap'n looked 'round on the crowd, and he see right away what they'd come for and what they was 'spectin' to see. Then he ordered the buoy hauled back and he got into the breeches himself, and we soused him through the surf and off he went to the brig. He showed her how to tuck her skirts in, and how to squat down in the breeches 'stead o' stickin' her feet through, and then she got skeered and said she couldn't and hollered, and so he got in with her and got his arms 'round her and landed her, both of 'em pretty wet." Saul stopped and leaned forward in his chair. I was evidently expected to say something.

"Well, that was just like the Captain," I said, mildly, "but where does the joke come in?"

"Well, there warn't no joke, really," remarked Saul with a wink around the room, " 'cept when we untangled 'em. She was 'bout seventy years old, and black as tar. That's all!"

It seemed to be my turn now—"the laugh" being on me. Captain Shortrode was evidently of the same opinion, for, on reentering the room, he threw the envelope on the table, and settling himself again in his chair looked my way, as if expecting the next break in the conversation to be made by me. Two surfmen, who had been asleep upstairs, now joined the group, the laughter over Saul's story of the "lady" having awakened them half an hour ahead of their time. They came in rubbing their eyes, their tarpaulins and hip-boots over their arms. Jerry, Tom, and Saul still remained tilted back in their chairs. They should have been in bed resting for their next patrol (they went out again at four A.M.), but preferred to sit up in my honor.

Dozens of stories flashed into my mind—the kind I would tell at a club dinner, or with the coffee and cigarettes—and were as instantly dropped. Such open-air, breezy giants, full of muscle and ozone, would find no interest in the adventures of

196

any of my characters; the cheap wit of the cafés,
the homely humor of the farm, the chatter of the
opera-box, or whisperings behind the palms of
the conservatory—nothing of this could possibly
interest these men. I would have been ashamed to
offer it. Tom's simple, straightforward story of
his baby and his brother Bill had made it impossible for me to attempt to match it with any
cheap pathos of my own; just as the graphic treat-
ment of the fitting out of the negro cook by the
Captain, and of the rescue of the "lady" by Saul,
had ended all hopes of my entertaining the men
around me with any worm-eaten, hollow-shelled
chestnuts of my own. What was wanted was some
big, simple, genuine yarn: strong meat for strong
men, not milk for babes: something they would
know all about and believe in and were part of.
The storming of a fort; the flagging of a train
within three feet of an abyss; the rescue of a child
along a burning ledge five stories above the sidewalk: all these themes bubbled up and sank again
in my mind. Some of them I only knew parts of;
some had but little point; all of them were hazy

197

in my mind. I remembered, with regret, that I could only repeat the first verse of the "Charge of the Light Brigade," and but two lines of "Horatius," correctly.

Suddenly a great light broke in upon me. What they wanted was something about their own life: some account of the deeds of other life-savers up and down the coast, graphically put with proper dramatic effect, beginning slowly and culminating in the third act with a blaze of heroism. These big, brawny heroes about me would then get a clearer idea of the estimation in which they were held by their countrymen; a clearer idea, too, of true heroism—of the genuine article, examples of which were almost nightly shown in their own lives. This would encourage them to still greater efforts, and the world thereby be the better for my telling.

That gallant rescue of the man off Quogue was just the thing!

The papers of the week before had been full of the bravery of these brother surfmen on the Long Island coast. This, and some additional information given me by a reporter who visited the scene of the disaster after the rescue, could not fail to make an impression, I thought. Yes, the rescue was the very thing.

"Oh! men," I began, "did you hear about that four-master that came ashore off Shinnecock last week?" and I looked around into their faces.

"No," remarked Jerry, pulling his pipe from his mouth. "What about it?"

"Why, yes, ye did," grunted Tom; "Number 17 got two of 'em."

"Yes, and the others were drowned," interrupted Saul.

"Thick, warn't it?" suggested one of the sleepy surfmen, thrusting his wharf-post of a leg into one section of his hip-boots preparatory to patrolling the beach.

"Yes," I continued, "dense fog; couldn't see five feet from the shore. She grounded about a mile west of the Station, and all the men had to locate her position by was the cries of the crew. They couldn't use the boat, the sea was running so heavy, and they couldn't get a line over her because they couldn't see her. They stood by, however, all night, and at daylight she broke in two. All that day the men of two stations worked to get off to them, and every time they were beaten back by the sea and wreckage. Then the fog cleared a little and two of the crew of the schooner were seen clinging to a piece of timber and some floating freight. Shot after shot was fired at them, and by a lucky hit one fell across them, and they made fast and were hauled toward the shore."

At this moment the surfman who had been struggling with his hip-boots caught my eye, nodded, and silently left the room, fully equipped for his patrol. I went on:

"When the wreckage, with the two men clinging to it, got within a hundred yards of the surf, the inshore floatage struck them, and smash they went into the thick of it. One of the shipwrecked men grabbed the line and tried to come ashore, the other poor fellow held to the wreckage. Twice the sea broke his hold, and still he held on."

The other surfman now, without even a nod, disappeared into the night, slamming the outer door behind him, the cold air finding its way into our warm retreat. I ignored the slight discourtesy and proceeded:

"Now, boys, comes the part of the story I think will interest you." As I said this I swept my glance around the room. Jerry was yawning behind his hand and Tom was shaking the ashes from his pipe.

"On the beach" (my voice rose now) "stood Bill Halsey, one of the Quogue crew. He knew that the sailor in his weakened condition could not hold on through the inshore wreckage; and sure enough, while he was looking, a roller came along and tore the man from his hold. In went Bill straight at the combers, fighting his way. There was not one chance in a hundred that he could live through it, but he got the man and held on, and the crew rushed in and hauled them clear of the smother, both of them half-dead, Bill's arms still locked around the sailor. Bill came to soonest, and the first words he said were, 'Don't mind me, I'm all right: take care of the sailor!' "

I looked around again; Captain Shortrode was examining the stubs of his horny fingers with as much care as if they would require amputation at no distant day; Jerry and Saul had their gaze on the floor. Tom was still tilted back, his eyes tight shut. I braced up and continued:

"All this, of course, men, you no doubt heard about, but what the reporter told me may be new to you. That night the 'Shipping News' got Bill on the 'phone and asked him if he was William Halsey."

" 'Yes.' "

" 'Are you the man who pulled the sailor out of the wreckage this morning at daybreak?' "

" 'Yes.' "

" 'Well, we'd like you to write some little account of——' "

" 'Well, I ain't got no time.' "

" 'If we send a reporter down, will you talk to him and——' "

" 'No, for there ain't nothin' to tell——' "

" 'You're Halsey, aren't you?' "

" 'Yes.' "

" 'Well, we should like to get some of the details; it was a very heroic rescue, and——' "

" 'Well, there ain't no details and there ain't no heroics. I git paid for what I do, and I done it,' " and he rang off the 'phone.

A dead silence followed—one of those uncomfortable silences that often follows a society break precipitating the well-known unpleasant quarter of an hour. This silence lasted only a minute. Then Captain Shortrode remarked calmly and coldly, and, I thought, with a tired feeling in his voice:

"Well, what else *could* he have said?"

The fur-coated beast was taken out of camphor, hooked up to the buggy, and the Captain and I ploughed our way back through the snow to the depot, the men standing in the door-way waving their hands Good-by.

The next day I wrote this to the Superintendent at headquarters:

"These men fear nothing but God!"

"OLD SUNSHINE"

"OLD SUNSHINE"

IT was when pulling in his milk one morning that Dalny first made the acquaintance of "Old Sunshine." The cans had become mixed, Dalny's pint having been laid at the old man's door and the old man's gill at Dalny's, and the rectifying of the mistake—"Old Sunshine" did the rectifying —laid the basis of the acquaintance.

Everybody, of course, in the Studio Building knew the old man and his old sister by sight, but only one or two well enough to speak to him; none of them to speak to the poor, faded woman, who would climb the stairs so many times a day, always stopping for her breath at the landing, and always with some little package—a pinch of tea, or a loaf of bread, or fragment of chop—which she hid under her apron if she heard anyone's steps. She was younger than her brother by a few years, but there was no mistaking their relationship; their noses were exactly alike—long, semi-transparent noses, protruding between two wistful, china-blue eyes peering from under eyebrows shaded by soft gray hair.

The rooms to which the sister climbed, and where the brother worked, were at the top of the building, away up under the corridor skylight, the iron ladder to its trap being bolted to the wall outside their very door. It was sunnier up there, the brother said. One of the rooms he used for his studio, sleeping on a cot behind a screen; the other was occupied by his sister. What little housekeeping was necessary went on behind this door. Outside, on its upper panel, was tacked a card bearing his name:

Adolphe Woolfsen.

When he had moved in, some years before— long before Dalny arrived in the building—the agent had copied the inscription in his book from this very card, and had thereafter nailed it to the panel to identify the occupant. It had never been removed, nor had any more important name-plate been placed beside it.

Sometimes the janitor, in addressing him, would call him "Mr. Adolphe," and sometimes "Mr. Woolfsen"; sometimes he would so far forget himself as to let his tongue slip half-way down "Old Sunshine," bringing up at the "Sun" and substituting either one of the foregoing in its place.

The agent who collected his rent always addressed him correctly. "If it was agreeable to Mr. Woolfsen, he would like to collect," etc. Sometimes it was agreeable to Mr. Woolfsen, and sometimes it was not. When it was agreeable—this the janitor said occurred only when a letter came with a foreign postmark on it—the old painter would politely beg the agent to excuse him for a moment, and shut the door carefully in the agent's face. Then would follow a hurried moving of easels and the shifting of a long screen across his picture. Then the agent would be received with a courteous bow and handed to a chair—a wreck of a chair, with the legs unsteady and the back wobbly, while the tenant would open an old desk, take a china pot from one of the cubby-holes, empty it of the contents, and begin to count out the money, smiling graciously all the time. When it was not agreeable to pay, the door was closed gently and silently in the agent's face, and no amount of pounding opened it again—not that day, at least.

Only Dalny knew what was behind that screen, and only Dalny divined the old man's reasons for concealing his canvas so carefully; but this was not until after weeks of friendly greeting, including certain attentions to the old sister, such as helping her up the stairs with a basket—an unusual occurrence for her, and, of course, for him. This time it was a measure of coal and a bundle of wood that made it so heavy.

"Thank you, sir," she had said in her sweet, gentle voice, her pale cheeks and sad eyes turned toward him; "my brother will be so pleased. No, I can't ask you in, for he is much absorbed these days, and I must not disturb him."

This little episode occurred only a few days after the incident of the interchange of the portions of milk, and was but another step to a foregone inti-

macy—so far as Dalny was concerned. Not that
he was curious, or lacked society or advice. It was
Dalny's way to be gracious, and he rarely had
cause to repent it. He did not pretend to any system of friendliness when meeting any fellow-lodger
on the stairs. It began with a cheery "Good-morning," or some remark about the weather, or a hope
that the water didn't get in through the skylight
and spoil any of his sketches. If a pleasant answer
came in response, Dalny kept on, and in a week
was lending brushes or tubes of color or a scuttle
of coal, never borrowing anything in return; if
only a gruff "Yes" or a nod of the head came
in reply, he passed on down or up the stairs
whistling as usual or humming some tune to himself. This was Dalny's way.

At first the painter's sobriquet of "Old Sunshine" puzzled Dalny; he saw him but seldom, but
never when his face had anything sunny about it.
It was always careworn and earnest, an eager, hungry look in his eyes.

Botts, who had the next studio to Dalny, solved
the mystery.

211

"He's crazy over a color scheme; gone daft on purples and yellows. I haven't seen it—nobody has except his old sister. He keeps it covered up, but he's got a 50×60 that he's worked on for years. Claims to have discovered a palette that will make a man use smoked glass when his picture is hung on the line. That's why he's called 'Old Sunshine.' "

Dalny made no reply, none that would encourage Botts in his flippant view of the old painter. He himself had been studying that same problem all his life; furthermore, he had always believed that sooner or later some magician would produce three tones—with harmonies so exact that a canvas would radiate light like a prism.

The next day he kept his studio-door open and his ear unbuttoned, and when the old man's steps approached his door on his return from his morning walk—the only hour he ever went out— Dalny threw it wide and stepped in front of him.

"Don't mind coming in, do you?" Dalny laughed. "I've struck a snag in a bit of drapery and can't get anything out of it. I thought you might help—" And before the old fellow could realize where he was, Dalny had him in a chair before his canvas.

"I'm not a figure-painter," the old man said, simply.

"That don't make any difference. Tell me what's the matter with that shadow—it's lumpy and flat," and Dalny pointed to a fold of velvet lying across a sofa, on which was seated the portrait of a stout woman—one of Dalny's pot-boilers—the wife of a rich brewer who wanted a picture at a poor price — one which afterward made Dalny's reputation, so masterful was the brushwork. The old Studio Building was full of just such customers, but not of such painters.

"It's of the old school," said the painter. "I could only criticise it in one way, and that might offend you."

"Go on—what is the matter with it?"

The old man rubbed his chin slowly and looked at Dalny under his bushy eyebrows.

"I am afraid to speak. You have been very kind.

My sister says you are always polite, and so few people are polite nowadays."

"Say what you please; don't worry about me. I learn something every day."

"No; I cannot. It would be cruel to tell you what I think, and Louise would not like it when she knew I had told you, and I must tell her. We tell each other everything."

"Is the color wrong?" persisted Dalny. "I've got the gray-white of the sky, as you see, and the reflected light from the red plush of the sofa; but the shadows between— Would you try a touch of emerald green here?"

The old man had risen from his seat now and was backing away toward the door, his hat in his hand, his bald head and the scanty gray hairs about his temples glistening in the overhead light of the studio.

"It would do you no good, my dear Mr. Dalny. Paint is never color. Color is an essence, a rhythm, a blending of tones as exquisite as the blending of sounds in the fall of a mountain-brook. Match each sound and you have its melody. Match each tone and you have light. I am working—working. Good-morning."

His hand was now on the door-knob, his face aglow with an enthusiasm which seemed to mingle with his words.

"Stop! Don't go; that's what I think myself," cried Dalny. "Talk to me about it."

The old man dropped the knob and looked at Dalny searchingly.

"You are honest with me?"

"Perfectly."

"Then when I triumph you shall see!—and you shall scc it first. I will come for you; not yet—not yet—perhaps to-morrow, perhaps next month— but I will come!" and he bowed himself out.

The faded sister was waiting for him at the top of the stairs. She had seen her brother mount the first flight and the fourth, all this by peering down between the banisters. Then he had disappeared. This, being unusual, had startled her.

"You must have stopped somewhere, Adolphe," she said, nervously.

"Yes, Louise; the painter on the floor below called me."

"Is he poor, like us?"

"Poorer. We have the light beyond. He has nothing, and never will have."

"What did he want?"

"A criticism."

"And you gave it?"

"No, I could not. I had not the heart to tell him. He tries so hard. He is honest, but his work is hopeless."

"Like the man on the first floor, who uses the calcium light to show his pictures by?"

"No, no; Mr. Dalny is a gentleman, not a cheat. He thinks, and would learn—he told me so. But he cannot see. Ah, not to see, Louise! Did you grind the new blue, dear? Yes—and quite smooth."

He had taken off his coat now, carefully, the lining being out of one sleeve. The sister hung it on a nail behind the door, and the painter picked up his palette and stood looking at a large canvas on an easel. Louise tiptoed out of the room and closed the door of her own apartment. When her brother began work she always left him alone. Triumph might come at any moment, and even a word wrongly spoken might distract his thoughts and spoil everything. She had not forgotten—nor ever would—how, two years before, she had come upon him suddenly just as an exact tint had been mixed, and, before he could lay it on his canvas, had unconsciously interrupted him, and all the hours and days of study had to be done over again. Now they had a system: when she must enter she would cough gently; then, if he did not hear her, she would cough again; if he did not answer, she would wait, sometimes without food, until far into the afternoon, when the daylight failed him. Then he would lay down his palette, covering his colors with water, and begin washing his brushes. This sound she knew. Only then would she open the door.

Botts had given Dalny the correct size of the canvas, but he had failed to describe the picture covering it. It was a landscape showing the sun setting behind a mountain, the sky reflected in a

lake; in the foreground was a stretch of meadow.
The sky was yellow and the mountain purple; the
meadow reddish brown. In the centre of the canvas was a white spot the size of a pill-box. This
was the sun, and the centre of the color scheme.
Radiating from this patch of white were thousands of little pats of chrome yellow and vermilion,
divided by smaller pats of blue. The exact grada-
tions of these tints were to produce the vibrations of light. One false note would destroy the
rhythm; hence the hours of thought and of end-
less trying.

These colors were not to be bought at the ordinary shops. Certain rare oxides formed the basis
of the yellows, while the filings of bits of turquoise
pounded to flour were used in the blues. Louise
did this, grinding the minerals by the hour, her
poor thin hands moving the glass pestle over the
stone slab. When some carefully thought-out tint
was laid beside another as carefully studied, the
combination meeting his ideal, he would spring
from his seat, crying out:

"Louise! Louise! Light! Light!"

Then the little woman would hurry in and stand entranced.

"Oh! so brilliant, Adolphe! It hurts my eyes to look at it. See how it glows! Ah, it will come!" and she would shade her wistful eyes with her hand as if the light from the flat canvas dazzled her. These were gala hours in the musty rooms at the top of the old Studio Building.

Then there would come long days of depression. The lower range of color was correct, but that over the right of the mountain and near the zenith did not pulsate. The fault lay in the poor quality of the colors or in the bad brushes or the sky outside. The faded sister's face always fell when the trouble lay with the colors. Even the small measure of milk would then have to be given up until the janitor came bearing another letter with a foreign stamp.

Dalny knew nothing of all this, nor did anyone else in the building—nothing positively of their home life—except from such outside indications as the size of the can of milk and the increasing shabbiness of their clothes. Dalny had suspected it and

219

had tried to win their confidence in his impulsive way; but all his advances had been met by a gentle, almost pathetic, reserve which was more insurmountable than a direct repulse. He also wanted to learn something more of the old man's methods. He had in his own earlier student days known an old professor in Heidelberg who used to talk to him about violet and green, but he never got any farther than talk. Here was a man, a German, too, perhaps —or perhaps a Swede—he could not tell from the name—some foreigner, anyhow—who was putting his theories into practice, and, more convincing still, was willing to starve slowly until they materialized.

Once he had cornered the old man on the stairs, and, throwing aside all duplicity, had asked him the straight question:

"Will you show me your picture? I showed you mine."

"Old Sunshine" raised his wide-brimmed hat from his head by the crown—it was too limp to be lifted in any other way—and said in a low voice:

"Yes, when it is a picture; it is now only an experiment."

"But it will help me if I can see your work. I am but a beginner; you are a master."

The good-natured touch of flattery made no impression on the old man.

"No," he answered, replacing his hat and keeping on his way downstairs, "I am not a master. I am a man groping in the dark, following a light that beckons me on. It will not help you; it will hurt you. I will come for you; I have promised, remember. Neither my sister nor I ever break a promise. Good-morning!" And again the shabby hat was lifted.

Dalny stood outside his own door listening to the old man's steps growing fainter until they reached the street; then he resumed his work on the green dress and puffy red face of the brewer's wife, correcting the errors he had made when she last sat for him, his mind unsatisfied, his curiosity all the more eager.

As the winter came on, Dalny began to miss the tread of the old man outside his door. The old sister never made any noise, so he never knew when she went up and down unless he happened to be on the stairs at the same moment. He knew the old man was at work, because he could hear his cease-less tramp before his easel—walking up to his pict-ure, laying on a pat of color, and walking back again. He himself had walked miles—had been do-ing it the day before in his efforts to give "carry-ing" quality to the shadow under the nose of the brewer's better half.

"I do not see your brother any more," Dalny had said to her one morning, after meeting her by accident outside his door carrying a basket with a cloth over it.

"No," she answered; "no; he cannot spare a moment these days. He hardly takes time to eat, and I do all the errands. But he is very happy." Here her face broke into a smile. "Oh, so happy! We both are——"

"And is the great picture finished?" he inter-rupted, with a movement as if to relieve her of the weight of the basket.

"Almost. . . . Almost. . . . Adolphe

will tell you when it is ready. No—please, good
Mr. Dalny—it is not heavy. But I thank you all
the same for wanting to help me. It is a little hot
soup for Adolphe. He is very fond of hot soup,
and they make it very nice at the corner."

The day following this interview Dalny heard
strange noises overhead. The steady tramping had
ceased; the sounds were as if heavy furniture was
being moved. Then there would come a pattering
of lighter feet running in and out of the connecting room. Then a noise as if scrubbing was being
done; he thought at one time he heard the splash
of water, and even looked up at his own ceiling
as if expecting a leak.

Suddenly these unusual sounds ceased, the old
man's door was flung open, a hurried step was
heard on the upper stairway, and a sharp knock
fell upon his own door.

Dalny opened it in the face of the old man. He
was bareheaded, his eyes blazing with excitement,
his face flushed as if by some uncontrollable joy.

"Come—quick!" he cried; "we are all ready. It
was perfected this morning. We have been putting

things in order for you, for we do not ever have guests. But you must be careful—your eyes are not accustomed, perhaps, and——"

Dalny darted back without listening to the old man's conclusion, and threw on his coat. The faded sister was upstairs, and he must be presentable.

"And you like your picture," burst out Dalny, as he adjusted his collar and cuffs—part of the old man's happiness had reached his own heart now.

"Like it? It is not something to *like*, Mr. Dalny. It is not a meal; it is a religion. You are in a fog, and the sun bursts through; you are in a tunnel, and are swept out into green fields; you grope in the dark, and an angel leads you to the light. You do not 'like' things then—you thank God on your knees. Louise has done nothing but cry."

These words came in shortened sentences divided by the mounting of each step, the two hurrying up the stairs, "Old Sunshine" ahead, Dalny following.

The sister was waiting for them at the open door. She had a snow-white kerchief over her shoulders and a quaint cap on her head, evidently her best. Her eyes, still red from weeping, shone like flashes of sunshine through falling rain.

"Keep him here, Louise, until I get my umbrella—I am afraid. No; stay till I come for you—" this to Dalny, who was, in his eagerness, peering into the well-swept, orderly looking room. "Shut your eyes until I tell you—quick! under this umbrella" (he had picked it up just inside the door).

Dalny suffered himself to be led into the room, his head smothered under the umbrella, the old man's hand firmly grasping his as if the distance between the door and the masterpiece was along the edge of an abyss.

"Now!" cried the old man, waving the umbrella aside.

Dalny raised his eyes, and a feeling of faintness came over him. Then a peculiar choking sensation crept into his throat. For a moment he did not and could not speak. The thousands of little patches of paint radiating from the centre spot were but so many blurs on a flat canvas. The failure was pathetic, but it was complete.

The old man was reading his face. The faded sister had not taken her eyes from his.

"It does not dazzle you! You do not see the vibrations?"

"I am getting my eyes accustomed to it," stammered Dalny. "I cannot take it all in at once." He was hunting around in his mind for something to say—something that would not break the old man's heart.

"No! You cannot deceive me. I had hoped better things of you, Mr. Dalny. It is not your fault that you cannot see."

The old man had crossed to the door of his studio, had thrown it open, and stood as if waiting for Dalny to pass out.

"Yes, but let me look a little longer," protested Dalny. The situation was too pathetic for him to be offended.

"No—no—please excuse us—we are very happy, Louise and I, and I would rather you left us alone.

226

I will come for you some other time—when my picture has been sent away. Please forgive my sister and me, but *please* go away."

Weeks passed before Dalny saw either one of the old people again. He watched for them, his door ajar, listening to every sound; but if they passed up and down the stairs, they did so when he was out or asleep. He had noticed, too, that all was still overhead, except a light tread which he knew must be the faded sister's. The heavier foot-fall, however, was silent.

One morning the janitor opened Dalny's door without knocking and closed it softly behind him. He seemed laboring under some excitement.

"He's up at St. Luke's Hospital; they took him there last night," he said in a whisper, jerking his thumb toward the ceiling.

"Who?"

" 'Old Sunshine.' "

"Crazy?"

"No; ill with fever; been sick for a week. Not bad, but the doctor would not let him stay here."

"Did the sister go?" There was a note of alarm in Dalny's voice.

"No, she is upstairs. That's why I came. I don't think she has much to eat. She won't let me in. Maybe you can get her to talk to you; she likes you—she told me so."

Dalny laid down his palette, tiptoed hurriedly up the stairs and knocked gently. There was no response. Then he knocked again, this time much louder, and waited. He heard the rustling of a skirt, but there was no other sound.

"It's Mr. Dalny, madam," he said in the kindest, most sympathetic voice that ever came out of his throat.

The door opened softly, and her face peered through the crack. Tears were in her eyes—old and new tears—following one another down her furrowed cheeks.

"He is gone away; they took him last night, Mr. Dalny." Her voice broke, but she still kept the edge of the door in her trembling hand.

"Yes; I have just heard about it. Let me come in, please; I want to help you. You are all alone."

Her grasp slackened, and Dalny stepped in.
The room was in some confusion. The bed where
her brother had been ill was still in disorder, the
screen that had concealed it pushed to one side.
On a table by his easel were the remains of a meal.
The masterpiece still stared out from its place.
The sister walked to a lounge and sat down.

"Tell me the truth," Dalny said, seating himself
beside her. "Have you any money?"

"No; our letter has not come."

"What do you expect to do?"

"I must sell something."

"Let me lend you some money. I have plenty,
for I shall get paid for my picture to-morrow;
then you can pay it back when yours comes."

"Oh, you are so kind, but we must sell something
of our own. We owe a large sum; the rent is two
months due, and there are other things, and
Adolphe must have some comforts. No, I am not
offended, but Adolphe would be if he knew."

Dalny looked into space for a moment, and
asked, thoughtfully, "How much do you owe?"

"Oh, a great deal," she answered, simply.

"What things will you sell?" At least he could help her in this.

The faded old lady looked up at Dalny and pointed to the masterpiece.

"It breaks our heart to send it away, but there is nothing else to do. It will bring, too, a great price; nothing else we possess will bring as much. Then we will have no more poverty, and someone may buy it who will love it, and so my brother will get his reward."

Dalny swept his eye around. The furniture was of the shabbiest; pictures and sketches tacked to the wall, but experiments in "Old Sunshine's" pet theories. Nothing else would bring anything. And the masterpiece! That, he knew, would not bring the cost of its frame.

"Where will you send it to be sold—to an art dealer?" Dalny asked. He could speak a good word for it, perhaps, if it should be sent to some dealer he knew.

"No; to a place in Cedar Street, where Adolphe sold some sketches his brother painters gave him in their student days. One by Achenbach—Oswald, not Andreas—brought a large sum. It was a great help to us. I have written the gentleman who keeps the auction-room, and he is to send for the picture to-morrow, and it will be sold in his next picture sale. Adolphe was willing; he told me to do it. 'Someone will know,' he said; 'and we ought not to enjoy it all to ourselves.' Then again, the problem has been solved. All his pictures after this will be full of beautiful light."

The auction-room was crowded. There was to be a sale of French pictures, some by the men of '30 and some by the more advanced impressionists. Many out-of-town buyers were present, a few of them dealers. Dalny rubbed his hands together in a pleased way when he looked over the audience and the collection. It was quite possible that some connoisseur newly made would take a fancy to the masterpiece, confounding it with some one of the pictures of the Upside-down School—pictures looking equally well whichever way they might be hung.

The selling began.

AT CLOSE RANGE

A Corot brought $2,700; a Daubigny, $940; two examples of the reigning success in Paris, $1,100. Twenty-two pictures had been sold.

Then the masterpiece was placed on the easel.

"A Sunrise. By Adolphe Woolfsen of Düsseldorf," called out the auctioneer. "What am I offered?"

There came a pause, and the auctioneer repeated the announcement.

A man sitting by the auctioneer, near enough to see every touch of the brush on "Old Sunshine's" picture, laughed, and nudged the man next to him. Several others joined in.

Then came a voice from behind:

"Five dollars!"

The auctioneer shrank a little, a pained, surprised feeling overspreading his face, as if someone had thrown a bit of orange-peel at him. Then he went on:

"Five dollars it is, gentlemen. Five—five—five!" Even he, with all the tricks of his trade at his fingers' ends, could not find a good word to say for "Old Sunshine's" masterpiece.

Dalny kept shifting his feet in his uneasiness. His hands opened and shut; his throat began to get dry. Then he broke loose:

"One hundred dollars!"

The auctioneer's face lighted up as suddenly as if the calcium light of the painter whom "Old Sunshine" despised had been thrown upon it.

"I have your bid, Mr. Dalny [he knew him]— one hundred — hundred — hundred — one — one —third and last call!"

Dalny thought of the gentle old face waiting at the top of the stairs, and of the old man's anxious look as he lay on his pillow. The auctioneer had seen Dalny's eager expression and at once began to address an imaginary bidder on the other side of the room—his clerk, really.

"Two hundred — two hundred — two — two — two——"

"Three hundred!" shouted Dalny.

Again the clerk nodded:

"Four—four!"

"Five!" shouted Dalny. This was all the money

he would get in the morning excepting fifty dollars—and that he owed for his rent.

"Five—five—five!—third and last call! SOLD! and to you, Mr. Dalny! Gentlemen, you seem to have been asleep. One of the most distinguished painters of our time is the possessor of this picture, which only shows that it takes an artist to pick out a good thing!"

She was waiting for him in her room, her own door ajar this time. He had promised to come back, and she was then to go to the hospital and tell the good news to her brother.

With his heart aglow with the pleasure in store for her, he bounded up the stairs, both hands held out, his face beaming:

"Wonderful success! Bought by a distinguished connoisseur who won't let the auctioneer give his name."

"Oh, I am so happy!" she answered. "That is really better than the money; and for how much, dear Mr. Dalny?"

"Five hundred dollars!"

"OLD SUNSHINE"

The faded sister's face fell.

"I thought it would bring a great deal more, but then Adolphe will be content. It was the lowest sum he mentioned when he decided to sell it. Will you go with me to tell him? Please do."

In the office of the hospital Dalny stopped to talk to the doctor, the sister going on up to the ward where "Old Sunshine" lay.

"Is he better?" asked Dalny. "He is a friend of mine."

The doctor tapped his forehead significantly with his forefinger.

"Brain trouble?" asked Dalny in a subdued tone.

"Yes."

"Will he get well?"

The doctor shook his head discouragingly.

"How long will he last?"

"Perhaps a week—perhaps not twenty-four hours."

The faded sister now entered. Her face was still smiling—no one had yet told her about her brother.

"Oh, he is so happy, Mr. Dalny."

235

AT CLOSE RANGE

"And you told him?"

"Yes! Yes!"

"And what did he say?"

"He put his arms around me and kissed me, and then he whispered, 'Oh! Louise, Louise! the connoisseur knew!'"

A POT OF JAM

A POT OF JAM

AFTER a fit of choking that could be heard all over the train the left lung of the locomotive gave out. I had heard her coughing up the long grade and had begun to wonder whether she would pull through, when she gave a wheeze and then a jerk, and out went her cylinder head.

Boston was four hours away and time of value to me. So it was to all the other passengers, judging from the variety and pungency of their remarks—all except one, an old lady who had boarded the train at a station near the foot of the long grade and who occupied a seat immediately in front of mine.

Such a dear old lady! plump and restful, a gray worsted shawl about her shoulders and a reticule on her arm. An old lady with a round rosy face framed in a hood-of-a-bonnet edged with ruffles, the strings tied under her chin, her two soft, human, kindly eyes peering at you over her gold-rimmed spectacles resting on the end of her nose. The sort of an old lady that you would like to have had for a mother provided you never had one of your own that you could remember—so comforting would have been her touch.

As the delay continued, the passengers made remarks. Some I cannot remember; others I cannot print.

One man in unblacked boots, with a full set of dusting-brush whiskers sticking up above his collarless shirt, smooth-shaven chin, red face, and a shock of iron-gray hair held in place by a slouch hat, said he'd "be doggoned if he ever knowed where he was at when he travelled on this road."

Another—a man with a leather case filled with samples on the seat beside him—a restless, loud-talking man, remarked that "they ought to build a cemetery at both ends of the road, and then the mourners could go in a walk and everybody would be satisfied, instead of trying to haul trains loaded with live people that wanted to get somewheres."

A POT OF JAM

Another—a woman this time, in a flower-covered hat and shiny brown silk dress, new, and evidently the pride of her heart from the care she took of it—one of those crisp, breezy, outspoken women of forty-five or fifty—slim, narrow-faced, keen-eyed, with a red—quite red—nose that would one day meet an ambitious upturned chin, and straight, firm mouth, the under lip pressed tight against the upper one when her mind was made up—remarked in a voice that sounded like a buzz-saw striking a knot:

"You ain't tellin' me that we're goin' to miss the train at Springfield, be ye?"

This remark being addressed to the car as a whole—no single passenger having vouchsafed any such information—was received in dead silence.

The arrival of the conductor, wiping the grease and grime from his hands with a wad of cotton-waste, revived hope for a moment and encouraged an air of gayety.

He was a gentlemanly conductor, patient, accustomed to be abused and brief in his replies.

"Maybe one hour; maybe six."

The gayety ceased.

The bewhiskered man said, "Well, I'll be gosh-durned!"

The sample-case man said, "—— —— ——
—— ——" (You can fill that up at your leisure.)

The woman in the brown silk rose to her feet, gathered her skirts carefully in her hand, skewered the conductor with her eye, and said: "You've gone and sp'ilt my day, that's what you've gone and done;" and, receiving no reply, crossed the aisle and plumped herself down in the overturned seat opposite the dear old lady, adding, as she shook out her skirt:

"Dirt mean, ain't it?"

The Dear Old Lady looked at the Woman in Brown, nodded in kindly assent, gazed at the conductor over her spectacles until he had closed the door, and said in a low, sweet voice that was addressed to nobody in particular, and yet which permeated the car like a strain of music:

"Well, if we're going to be here for six hours I guess I'll knit."

Just here I began to be interested. The philos-

ophy of the dear woman's life had evidently made
her proof against such trivialities. Six hours! What
difference did it make? There was a flavor of the
Mañana por la mañana of the Spaniard and the
Dolce far niente of the Italian in her acceptance of
the situation that appealed to me. Another sun
would rise on the morrow as beautiful as the one
we had to-day; why worry over its setting? Let
us eat, drink, and be merry—or knit. It was all the
same to her.

I immediately wanted to know more of this passenger—a desire that did not in the slightest degree
extend to any other inmate of the car. And yet
there were restrictions and barriers which I could
not pass. Not occupying the seat beside her or
opposite her, but the one behind her, I, of course,
was not on terms of such intimacy as would make it
possible for me to presume upon her privacy. She
was occupying her own house, as it were, framed in
between two seat-backs turned to face each other,
giving her the use of four seats—one of which had
been usurped by the Woman in Brown. I had my
one seat with my bag beside me, giving me the

243

privileges of two sittings. Between us, of course, was the back of her own seat, over which I looked and studied her back hair and bonnet and shawl and—knitting.

Under the circumstances I could no more intrude upon the Dear Old Lady's privacy than upon a neighbor's who lived next door to me but whom I did not know and was separated from me only by an eight-inch brick wall. The conventionalities of life enforce these conditions. When, therefore, the Dear Old Lady informed me and the car that she would "knit," I got myself into position to watch the operation; not obtrusively, not with any intention of prying into her private life, but just because—well, just because I couldn't help it.

There was something about her, somehow, that I could not resist. I knew a Dear Old Lady once. She wasn't so stout as this old lady and her eyes were not brown, but blue, and her hair smooth as gray satin and of the same color. I can see her now as I write, the lamplight falling on her ivory needles and tangle of white yarn—and sometimes, even now, I think I hear her voice.

A POT OF JAM

The Dear Old Lady before me felt in her pocket, pulling up her overskirt and fumbling about for a mysterious pouch that was tied around her waist, perhaps, and in which she carried her purse, and then she pinched her reticle and said to herself— I was so near I could hear every word: "Oh, I guess I put it in the bag"—and she leaned over and began unfastening the clasps of an old-fashioned carpet-bag, encased in a pocket-edition of a linen duster, which rested on the seat in front of her and beside the Woman in Brown, who drew her immaculate, never-to-be-spotted silk skirt out of the way of any possible polluting touch.

I craned my head. Somehow I could hardly wait to see what kind of knitting she would take out— whether it was a man's stocking or a baby's mitten or a pair of wee socks, or a stripe to sew in an afghan to put over somebody's bed. What stories could be written about the things dear old ladies knit—what stories they are, really! In every ball of yarn there is a thread that leads from one heart to another: to some big son or fragile daughter, or to the owner of a pair of pink toes that won't stay covered no matter how close the crib—or to a chubby-faced boy with frost-tipped ears or cheeks.

First came the ball of yarn—just plain gray yarn—and then two steel needles, and then——

Then the Dear Old Lady stopped, and an expression of blank amazement overspread her sweet face as her fingers searched the interior of the bag.

"Why," she said to herself, "why! Well! You don't tell me that—well! I never knew that to happen before. Oh, isn't that dreadful! Well, I *never!*" Here she drew out an unfinished gray yarn stocking. "Just look at it! Isn't it awful!"

The Woman in Brown sprang to her feet and switched her dress close to her knees.

"What is it?" she cried.

"Jam!" answered the old lady.

"Jam! You don't mean to say——"

"That's just what it is. Blackberry jam, that my Lizzie put up for John just before I left home and —oh, isn't it too bad! It's streaming all over the seat and running down on the floor! Oh my! my!"

The Woman in Brown gave a bound and was out in the aisle. "Well, I should think," she cried indignantly, "that you'd had sense enough to know better than to carry jam in a thing like that. I ain't got none on me, hev I?"

The Dear Old Lady didn't reply. She was too much absorbed in her own misfortunes to notice her companions.

"I told Lizzie," she continued, "just 'fore I left, that she oughter put it in a basket, but she 'lowed that it had a tin cap and was screwed tight, and that she'd stuff it down in my clothes and it would carry all right. I ain't never left it out of my hand but once, and then I give it to the man who helped me up the steps. He must have set it down sudden like."

As she spoke she drew out from the inside of the bag certain articles of apparel which she laid on the seat. One—evidently a neck handkerchief—looked like a towel that had just wiped off the face of a boy who had swallowed the contents of the jar.

The Woman in Brown was in the aisle now examining her skirts, twisting them round and round in search of stray bits of jam. The Dear Old Lady was still at work in her bag, her back shielding its smeared contents. Trickling down upon the floor and puddling in the aisle and under the seats on the opposite side of the car ran a sticky fluid that the woman avoided stepping upon with as much care as if it had been a snake.

I started forward to help, and then I suddenly checked myself. What could I do? The blackberry jam had not only soaked John's stockings, but it had also permeated. Well, the Dear Old Lady was travelling and evidently on the way to see John—her son, no doubt—and to stay all night. No, it was beyond question; I could not be of the slightest use. Then again, there was a woman present. Whatever help the Dear Old Lady needed should come from her.

"You ain't got no knife, I suppose?" I heard the Woman in Brown say. "If you had you could scrape most of it off."

"No," answered the Dear Old Lady. "Have you?"

"Well, I did hev, but I don't just know where it is. It would gorm that up, too, maybe, if I did find it."

A POT OF JAM

"No, I guess the best way is to try and wash it off. I'll get rid of this anyway," the Dear Old Lady answered; and out came the treacherous jar with the crack extending down its side, its metal top loose, the whole wrapped in yellow paper—all of which she dropped out of the open window.

During this last examination the Woman in Brown stood in the aisle, her skirts above her ankles. It wasn't her bag, or her stockings, or her jam. She had paid her fare and was entitled to her seat and its surrounding comforts: I had a good view of her face as she stood in front of me, and I saw what was passing in her mind. To this air of being imposed upon, first by the railroad and now by this fellow-passenger, was added a certain air of disgust—a contempt for any one, however old, who could be so stupid and careless. The little wrinkles that kept puckering at the base of her red lobster-claw of a nose—it really looked like one—helped me in this diagnosis. Its shape prevented her from turning it up at anybody, and wrinkling was all that was left. Having read her thoughts as reflected in her face, I was no longer surprised that she continued standing without offering in any way to help her companion out of her dilemma.

The Dear Old Lady's examination over, and the intricacies of her bag explored and the corners of certain articles of apparel lifted and immediately replaced again, she said to herself, with a sigh of relief:

"Ain't but one stocking tetched, anyhow. Most of it's gone into my shoes—yes, that's better. Oh, I was so scared!"

"Everything stuck up, ain't it?" rasped the Woman. She hadn't taken her seat yet. It seemed to me she could get more comfort out of the Old Lady's misery standing up.

"Well, it might ha' been worse, but I ain't goin' to worry a mite over it. I'll go to the cooler and wash up what I can, and the rest's got to wait till I get to John's," she said in her sweet, patient way, as she gathered up the bag and its contents and made her way to the wash-basin.

The car relapsed into its former dull condition. Those of the passengers who were not experts and whose advice, if taken, would have immediately replaced the cylinder-head and sent the train in on time, were picking flowers outside the track, but close enough to the train to spring aboard at the first sign of life in the motive-power. Every now and then there would come a back-thrust of the car and a bumping into the one behind us. Some scientist who had spent his life in a country store hereupon explained to a mechanical engineer who had a market garden out of Springfield (I learned this from their conversation) that "it was the b'iler that acted that way; the engineer was lettin' off steam and the jerk come when he raised the safety-valve."

A brakeman now opened the door nearest the water-cooler, passed the old lady washing up, ran amuck through a volley of questions fired at him in rapid succession, and slammed the other door behind him without replying to one of them. In this fusillade the Woman in Brown, who had now turned over a flower-picking passenger's seat in addition to her own, had managed her tongue with the rapidity and precision of a Gatling gun.

One of those mysterious rumors, picked up from

251

some scrap of conversation heard outside, now drifted through the car. It conveyed the information that another engine had been telegraphed for and would be along soon. This possibility the Sample-Case Man demolished by remarking in his peculiar vernacular—unprintable, all of it—that it was ten miles to the nearest telegraph station and it would take two hours to walk it.

The bottom having dropped out of this slight hope, the car relapsed into its dull monotony. No statement now of any kind would be believed by anybody.

During this depression I espied the Dear Old Lady making her way down the aisle. No trace of anxiety was on her face. The bag had resumed its former appearance, its linen duster buttoned tight over its ample chest.

The Woman in Brown was waiting for her, her feet up on the flower-picking passenger's seat, her precious brown silk tucked in above her shoes.

"Quite a muss, warn't it?" she said with rather a gleeful tone, as if she rejoiced in the Old Lady's punishment for her stupidity.

"Yes, but it's all right now. It soaked through my shoes and went all over my cap, and—" Here she bent her head and whispered into the Woman's ear. I realized then how impossible it would have been for me to have rendered the slightest assistance.

She had taken her seat now and had laid the bag in its original position on the cushion in front of her. My heart had gone out to her, but I was powerless to help. Once or twice I conned over in my mind an expression of sympathy, but I could not decide on just what I ought to say and when I ought to say it, and so I kept silent. I should not have felt that way about the Woman in Brown, who sat across from me, her two feet patting away on the seat cushion as if to express her delight that she had escaped the catastrophe (toes express joy oftener than fingers, if we did but know it). It would not have taken me five seconds to express my opinion of her—with my toes had she been a man.

The Dear Old Lady began now to rearrange her toilet, drawing up her shawl, tightening the strings of her comfortable bonnet, wiping the big gold spectacles on a bit of chamois from her reticule. I watched every movement. Somehow I could not keep my eyes from her. Then I heard her say in a low voice to herself:

"Well, the toe warn't stained—I guess I can work on that."

Out came the needles and yarn again, and the wrinkled fingers settled down to their work. No more charming picture in the world than the one now before me!

The Woman in Brown held a different opinion. Craning her head and getting a full view of the Dear Old Lady peacefully and comfortably at work, all her sorrows ended, she snapped out:

"I s'pose ye don't know I can't put my feet down nowheres. It's all a muck round here; you seed it when the jar fust busted, 'cause I heard ye say so. I been 'spectin' ye'd clean it up somehow."

Down went the knitting and up she got.

"Oh, I'm so sorry. I'll get a newspaper and wipe it up. I hope you didn't get none on your clothes."

A POT OF JAM

"Oh, I took care o' that! This is a brand-new dress and I ain't wore it afore. I don't get nothin' on *my* clothes—I ain't that kind." This last came with a note of triumph in her voice.

I watched the Dear Old Lady lean over the thin axe-handle ankles of the Woman in Brown, mop up a little pool of jam-juice, tuck the stained paper under the crossbar, and regain her seat. I started up to help, but it was all over before I could interfere.

The Dear Old Lady resumed her knitting. The Woman in Brown put down her feet; her rights had been recognized and she was satisfied. I kept up my vigil.

Soon a movement opposite attracted me. I raised my eyes. The Woman in Brown, with her eye on the Dear Old Lady, was stealthily opening a small paper bundle. She had the air of a boy watching a policeman. The paper parcel contained a red napkin, a dinner knife, and two fat sandwiches streaming with butter.

"Oh, you brought your lunch with you, did ye?" remarked the Dear Old Lady, who had unexpectedly raised her eyes from her knitting and at the wrong moment.

"Well, jes' a bite. I'd offer ye some, but I heard ye say that you were goin' to eat dinner with your son. That's so, ain't it?"

"Yes, that's so."

The needles kept on their course, the Dear Old Lady's thoughts worked in with every stitch. It was now twelve o'clock, and Boston hours away. John would dine late if he waited for his old mother.

The red napkin had now been laid on the seat cushion and the sandwiches placed side by side in full sight of the car. Concealment was no longer necessary.

"I don't s'pose ye left any water in the cooler, did ye?"

"Oh, plenty," came the reply, the needles still plying, the dear face fixed on their movement.

"Well, then, I guess before I eat I'll get a cup," and she covered the luncheon with the brown paper and passed down the aisle.

During her brief absence several important in-

cidents took place. First there came a jerk that felt
for a moment like a head-on collision. This was a
new locomotive, which had been sent to our relief,
butting into the rear car. Then followed a rush of
passengers, flower-pickers, mechanical engineers,
scientists, sample-case man, and, last, the man
with the dusting-brush whiskers. He paused for a
moment, located his seat by his umbrella in the rack
overhead, picked up the paper parcel, transferred
it to the other seat, the one the woman in Brown
had just left, tilted forward the back, and sat
down.

When he had settled himself and raised his head,
the Woman in Brown stood over him looking into
his eyes, an angry expression on her face. She held
a cup of water in her hand.

"My seat, ain't it?" he blurted out.

"Yes, 'spec' it is," she snarled back, "long as
you want it." And she gathered her skirts carefully,
edged into the reduced space of her former seat,
laid the cup of water on the sill of the window, and
sat down as carefully as a hen adjusting herself

to a nest, and, I thought, with precisely the same movement.

A moment more and she leaned over the seat-back and said to the bewhiskered man:

"Hand me that napkin and stuff, will ye?"

The man moved his arm, picked up his newspaper, looked under it, and said:

"It ain't here."

"Well, I guess it is. I sot it there not more'n two minutes ago!"

The man settled himself in his seat and began to read.

"Look 'round there, will ye? Maybe it dropped on the floor."

"It ain't on the floor. Guess I know a napkin when I see it." This came with some degree of positiveness.

"Well, it ain't here. I left it right where you're a-sittin' when I went and got this water. You ain't eat it, hev ye?" She was still in her seat, her head twisted about, her face expressing every thought that crossed her mind.

"No, I ain't eat it. I ain't no goat!" and the

man buried his face in his paper. For him the incident was closed.

Here there came a still small voice floating out from the lips of the Dear Old Lady, slowly, one word at a time:

"Ain't you set on it?"

"Set on it! *What!*"

She was on her feet now, pulling her skirt around, craning her neck, her face getting whiter and whiter as the truth dawned upon her.

"Oh, Lordy! Jes' look at it! However did I come to! Oh!"

"Here, take my handkerchief," murmured the Dear Old Lady. "Let me help wipe it off." And she laid down her knitting.

Oh, but it was a beautiful stain! A large, irregular, map-like stain, with the counties plotted in bits of ham and the townships in smears of bread, with little rivers of butter running everywhere. One dear, beloved rill in an ectasy of delight had skipped a fold and was pushing a heap of butter ahead of it down a side plait.

I hugged myself with the joy of it all. If it had

only been a crock she had sat in, with sandwiches enough to supply a picnic!

And the stain!

That should have been as large as the State of Rhode Island!